Once Upon a Christmas Miracle

By

Frank Cereo

Frank Cereo

Contents

Chapter 1 – Thanksgiving Dinner

It's a cold dreary day as Cheryl prepares to baste the Thanksgiving Day turkey. The rain outside, makes it feel cool and damp inside the house. Cheryl uses the ladle and slowly pours the natural juices over the turkey. The smell of the turkey cooking is infiltrating throughout the entire house. Today is the beginning of the holiday season and Cheryl wants to make sure everything goes well. She knows she has to invite her mother-in-law over and she always criticizes Cheryl's cooking. Today Cheryl wants to impress her mother-in-law Gracie. She wants to make sure everything is perfect including the creamy mashed potatoes. Cheryl continues to prepare the dinner when her husband Todd comes out of the bedroom.

"Good morning, how did you sleep last night?" Cheryl asks Todd as she kisses him on the cheek.

"I didn't sleep too well. I was restless, tossing and turning all night." Todd replies as he pours himself a cup of coffee.

Todd and Cheryl have been married for thirteen years. They have two children. Danielle, their daughter, is thirteen years old and she was the reason why they got married. They also have a son Michael, who is eight years old. Their marriage has been up and down kind of like most middle-class couples. It was tough when they first got married because money was tight and the new baby took a lot of their time. Cheryl is a short thin woman and at the age of thirty-four, she is still quite beautiful. She has long auburn hair that comes down to her shoulder blades. She also has big brown eyes with very long eyelashes. Her figure still resembles her high school cheerleading days, even though she has put on about ten pounds. After the children were born, Cheryl stayed home and took care of them until Michael started school three years ago. When Michael started school, Cheryl went back to work as a cashier at a large grocery chain. Last year Cheryl was promoted to customer service associate and works behind the customer service desk. She only makes $10 an hour, which helps pay the bills and puts groceries on the table.

"What time is your mother coming over?" Cheryl asks Todd as she ducks her head into the living room.

"You know her, she is always early." Todd replies as he changes the channel to the Thanksgiving Day Parade.

Todd on the other hand, is tall and lanky. He stands over six feet tall and weighs about one hundred eighty-five pounds. Todd is four years older than Cheryl. He has long dark hair that is slicked back and matted down with hair cream. Todd sports a mustache that is very thin and looks like peach fuzz. Todd on the other hand, works at a car dealership and he is the bread winner of the family. He is a sales representative and he likes to talk. Todd makes a pretty good living selling two or three cars a week. He is very flirtatious and likes to flirt with all the young women that come in to buy a car. Even though Todd and Cheryl have been married for thirteen years, they seem to be growing apart. Over the past couple of years, Todd and Cheryl hardly ever make love. Todd is always working late into the evening and doesn't have time for her. Life has been hard but they have managed their differences because of the children.

"Hey Todd, can you watch the turkey while I take my shower?" Cheryl asks.

"Yeah, yeah no problem." Todd replies as he takes a sip of his coffee.

Cheryl goes into the bathroom and washes up. She dries off and brushes her teeth. She pulls her hair back and puts it in a ponytail. She applies her makeup and dresses nicely for the holiday. Today Cheryl decides she is going to where a pretty white sweater and a short pink skirt. She is trying to rekindle her romance with Todd. She even wears a garter belt with stockings, trying to entice her husband on a romantic evening. Cheryl walks out into the kitchen and smells something burning.

"I ask you to do one thing and you can't get off your lazy butt to baste the turkey." Cheryl says with anger.

"I checked it and it was fine" Todd yells back at Cheryl.

"You know Todd, all I wanted to do is impress your mother, just once." Cheryl replies angrily as she bastes the turkey.

The morning goes by quickly and Cheryl prepares dinner. Both children soon arrive in the living area after their slumbers. Danielle is the first to arrive. She is wearing a purple sweater and a pair of jeans. Danielle is a spitting image of her mother with one exception, she has dark brown hair. Danielle is in eighth grade and she is a straight A student. She is a good girl and hardly ever gets into trouble. She helps her mother out when she is asked and she always keeps her room clean. When Danielle comes into the kitchen, she goes right for the refrigerator. She grabs the orange juice and pours herself a glass.

"My God mom, the turkey sure smells delicious." Danielle says as she takes a sip of her orange juice.

"Thanks honey, I sure hope it tastes as good as it smells." Cheryl replies with a smile.

"Mom, you always make an awesome Thanksgiving dinner." Danielle responds as she walks into the living room.

Cheryl smiles at her daughter Danielle because she has been the highlight of her life. Even though Danielle is only thirteen years old, she acts ten years her senior. Danielle takes a seat on the sofa next to her father. Cheryl remains in the kitchen preparing the potatoes and vegetables. While she is peeling the potatoes, Michael comes thundering down the stairs. He walks into the kitchen and grabs a bowl for his cereal.

"Good morning Michael. How did you sleep?" Cheryl asks.

"I slept good mom, the only thing that bothered me was the dog. He wouldn't sit still and kept rolling from side to side on the bed." Michael replies with a smile.

"Michael, how many times have I told you do not to let the dog sleep on your bed?" Cheryl responds.

Michael on the other hand, is eight years old. He is short for his age and he will grow in time. Michael is also a little overweight and wears his hair high and tight, like he is in the military. Michael is a normal eight-year-old but he suffers from a learning disorder. He has to take special classes in school to help him. With his learning disorder, Michael finds himself the victim of bullying in school. Michael does his best and tries to ignore the bullies in school, but they always find a way to get under his skin. The teachers and principle do their best to try and protect Michael, but there's always an opportunity for the other children find him vulnerable.

At 2:30 in the afternoon, Todd's mother Gracie arrives. Even though dinner is at 4 o'clock, Gracie always arrives early. Gracie stands about four feet eight inches tall and smokes like a chimney. She is sixty-two years old and wears her salt-and-pepper hair in a perm. Gracie has never been fond of Cheryl and she continually calls her a gold digger. Gracie always gets a jab in about how Cheryl planned to get pregnant, so Todd would have to marry her. All in all, Gracie really despises Cheryl. She would do anything to get Todd away from her. When Gracie walks in she is carrying two pies. One pumpkin and the other one apple. When she walks into the kitchen she carries the pies over to the refrigerator and puts them in.

"Grandma, grandma," Michael says as he comes running towards Gracie with open arms.

"Hi pumpkin, how are you?" Gracie says as she wraps her arms around Michael.

Danielle walks in and gives Gracie a hug and kiss. Todd remain seated on the sofa. Right away Gracie opens her purse and takes out a non-filtered Pall Mall cigarette.

"Mom, I really would appreciate you not smoking in front of the children." Cheryl pleads.

"Well Cheryl, I would really appreciate you not calling me mom because I'm not your mother. Besides the children don't mind if I smoke." Gracie replies with attitude.

This type of behavior really upsets Cheryl because she doesn't even feel welcome in her own home. Cheryl blows it off quickly and prepares dinner. Gracie doesn't even bother to ask Cheryl if she needs any help. Gracie goes right into the living room and sits next to Todd. Just before four o'clock, Cheryl calls everyone to the table because dinner is ready. The table looks immaculate with candles and flowers. Todd sits at the head of the table and carves the turkey. The turkey is cooked to perfection and it slices so easily as the juices drip into the plate. The dinner is served home style as everything is passed around. Cheryl pours the wine into her glass, and then she fills Gracie and Todd's glass. Cheryl takes her seat and prepares to say grace. After grace, the group of five begins to eat.

"How long did you cook the turkey, twelve to fifteen hours?" Gracie asks in an ill-mannered way.

"What are you talking about Gracie? The turkey is cooked to perfection." Cheryl replies.

"You're full of it Cheryl, it's dry and tastes like crap." Gracie answers with a snotty tone.

"She is right honey, the turkey is dry." Todd says in despair.

Cheryl is beside herself because no matter what she does, she cannot please her mother-in-law. She knows there is nothing wrong with the turkey. Gracie has to find something to complain about. What's worst of all, is Todd backs her up. Cheryl is so pissed off, she is ready to hammer back but holds her tongue as she lets it slide. After dinner, Todd and Gracie go back into the living room to watch the football games. Michael goes upstairs to play video games. Cheryl not only cooked feast but she also has to clean up the mess.

"Need some help mom?" Danielle asks.

"Sure kiddo, mom can always use a little help." Cheryl replies

Cheryl and Danielle pick up all the dirty plates and put them into the dishwasher. Cheryl hand washes all the pots and pans, while Danielle dries them and puts them away. When the decks are cleared, Cheryl serves the pies. Again they all go back to the table where the pies are served with coffee. Cheryl pulls out a can of whipped cream and sets it on the table.

"You mean to say were not having fresh whipped cream?" Gracie rumbles out.

Cheryl is beside herself and doesn't know what to say. Every other year Gracie brings the fresh whipped cream already whipped. Cheryl knows whatever she says, Gracie is going to have a smartass remark about it. Cheryl pours the coffee and takes a seat at the table. Cheryl uses her fork and cuts into her piece of pumpkin pie.

"So are you going shopping on Black Friday?" Gracie asks Cheryl.

"Maybe, I have to work all day tomorrow. I might go out for a few hours after work." Cheryl replies.

"Yeah go ahead and spend all my son's money. He works so hard and you spend so easily." Gracie says with an evil voice.

The evening goes by quickly and Gracie prepares to go home. She gives Todd a big hug and kiss while bending down to give Danielle and Michael a peck on the cheek. Cheryl empties the dishwasher and reloads it with the dessert dishes. She runs the dishwasher and cleans off the stove, before sitting down in the living room. Cheryl sits right next to Todd on the sofa as they watch the final football game of the night.

"Hey, are there any Christmas specials on tonight?" Cheryl asks Todd.

"You want to watch Christmas specials, go into the bedroom and watch them. I'm watching the football game." Todd replies firmly.

Cheryl disregards Todd's comment and puts her head back and falls asleep. She wakes up when she hears Todd yelling and screaming at the TV because of a bad call in the football game. Cheryl looks at the clock and sees its getting close to 11:30. She looks around the room and notices the children have already gone to bed. That's when she remembers all the sexy lingerie that she wore underneath her skirt. Cheryl was in a romantic mood and starts to flirt with Todd. She slowly and seductively pulls up her skirt to show her upper thigh. She shows Todd her black stocking tops and the lace of her white slip. Todd sits there emotionless as Cheryl starts to rub his leg.

"Enough of that nonsense. I'm going to bed, I have to work in the morning. Tomorrow's Black Friday and it's going to be a big sales day." Todd says as he gets up from the sofa.

"I thought maybe you and I could have a romantic evening." Cheryl says as she gets up and turns off the TV.

Cheryl walks over and turns off all the lights and follows Todd upstairs as he goes into their bedroom. She closes the door behind her and Todd quickly strips off his clothes. Cheryl goes into the master bath and brushes her teeth. When she comes out of the bathroom, the lights are all off in the bedroom. Todd is under the covers and getting comfortable in the bed. She starts to take off her clothes in a seductive way and Todd looks the other way.

"What's wrong? Did I do something wrong?" Cheryl pleads.

"No, I'm just tired. Get undressed and let's go to sleep." Todd replies as he rolls over on his side.

Cheryl undresses and puts away all her sexy lingerie. She is disgusted with her husband's attitude and behavior for the entire day. She cooked a fantastic meal and she was ridiculed by her mother-in-law. She dressed up seductively for her husband and he blew her off. This wasn't the way Cheryl anticipated the day to go. Cheryl quickly dresses in a flannel night shirt. She gets into bed and lays next to her was her husband.

"Your mother was very rude today. I thought everything was cooked to perfection." Cheryl says to Todd.

"You know how she is, why do you let it bother you? Just go to sleep, we both have to work in the morning." Todd replies.

"You know she's hated me all along. We've given her two beautiful grandchildren and I still can't believe the way she treats me. She is a selfish and crude person." Cheryl says.

"It's just your imagination. Now go to sleep." Todd replies as he pulls his pillow over his ears.

Cheryl watches as Todd pulls the pillow around his head. She is disgusted with his attitude and his mother's behavior. The plan for a perfect day goes down the drain as Cheryl stares up at the ceiling. Within minutes, Todd is snoring like a buzz saw. His behavior has been going downhill for the past three to four months. Cheryl notices his sex drive is gone and he doesn't even look twice at her anymore. She knows something is wrong and tomorrow she needs to find out what that problem is. Cheryl rolls over on her side and begins to cry. She can feel the teardrops while they roll down her cheek. Cheryl ends up crying herself to sleep.

Chapter 2 – Black Friday

The next morning, Cheryl wakes up at six. She takes her shower and gets dressed for work. Today is a casual day, so she gets to wear jeans and a sweatshirt. Cheryl is working from seven to four and Todd is working from nine in the morning until eleven in the evening. The kids are spending the day at Grandma Gracie's house. After work Cheryl makes arrangements with Gracie to watch the kids so she can get some Christmas shopping done. Black Friday makes for a long and hectic day at work with so many people out shopping. Cheryl is working at the customer service desk with hundreds of people asking questions. They are asking for change, bringing in bottle returns, and she is keeping up a relentless pace. By three o'clock Cheryl is clock watching. Her feet are killing her because she has been on them all day. By four o'clock Cheryl practically runs to the time clock. She punches out and makes her out to the car. Cheryl drives down to the mall. This is perfect timing to buy Danielle and Michael a few gifts. Danielle has stated that she really wants an iPhone. Michael on the other hand, has been hinting about a new Xbox. Cheryl's first stop is the Verizon store in the mall. She looks around at all the different iPhones and can't make up her mind. She knows Danielle also wants the iPhone to include an iPod for music. She finally finds the one that Danielle will like. Cheryl makes sure it has a pink cover because that is Danielle's favorite color. After everything is set, Cheryl hands the clerk her debit card. Cheryl waits patiently for the clerk to run her card because she wants to get to Game Stop and get Michael's his Xbox. The clerk takes a few extra minutes and returns with her debit card and hands it back to her.

"This card was denied. Do you have another card?" The clerk asks.

"That can't be. I just got paid today and I received my bonus too." Cheryl says as she looks in her purse for her credit card.

"Do you have another credit card or cash?" The clerk asks.

"Here, try my credit card. I will have to call my bank and find out what's going on with my debit card." Cheryl says in disgust.

The clerk tries to run Cheryl's credit card and it's denied both times.

"This card is no good either. It's been denied." The clerk says.

"Can you please hang on to this? I'll be back shortly after I find out what's going on." Cheryl asks.

"I'll hang on to it until closing tonight. Then I will have to put it back into stock." The clerk replies.

Cheryl leaves the mall disgusted. She knows she just got paid over $400 including her pay and bonus. There has to be a banking problem. She looks at her watch and notices it after six and the banks are closed. Cheryl knows she will have to take care of the problem tomorrow. Cheryl gets into her car and heads to her mother-in-law's house. She knocks on the door and Gracie lets her in.

"How did your shopping spree go?" Gracie asks sarcastically.

"Couldn't get anything there is something wrong with my debit card. I will have to check with the bank tomorrow morning." Cheryl says dejectedly.

"Oh really, well you better get that taken care of immediately!" Gracie says in an ill-mannered tone.

Cheryl and her two kids head home. She parks the car in the driveway. They get out of the car and go into the house. Cheryl walks in first, followed by Danielle and Michael. She looks around and to her surprise all the furniture is gone. Cheryl picks up her cell phone and calls Todd at the car dealership.

"Hello, Putnam car sales, this is Louise how can I help you?" Louise says.

"Hi Louise, this is Cheryl LaRussa, is Todd there?" Cheryl asks.

"Hi Cheryl, Todd resigned a couple of weeks ago and his last day was Wednesday." Louise stutters to get the words out.

"What are you talking about? This is news to me. I came home to an empty house. What is going on?" Cheryl asks frantically.

"I'm sorry Cheryl, I have no clue where he went." Louise replies.

Cheryl hangs up the cell phone without saying goodbye. Then she calls Todd's cell phone and it goes right to voicemail. Cheryl calls over and over again and the phone continues to go to voicemail. Cheryl is beside herself and before she begins to panic she calls Gracie. Cheryl dials the number with tears dripping from her eyes. She doesn't know what's happing and she is scared. The phone begins to ring and Gracie picks it up it up on the second ring.

"Hello," Gracie says.

"Gracie, its Cheryl. Do you know where Todd is?" Cheryl asks in a broken up voice from crying.

"Ahh honey, he left town and he won't be coming back." Gracie replies.

"What do you mean?" Cheryl asks with concern.

"He decided it was time to move on." Gracie says.

"Move on with what or should I say with who?" Cheryl asks.

"Never mind with who. Just look on your kitchen counter and you will find the paperwork." Gracie says.

Cheryl walks into the kitchen without saying another word to Gracie. On the counter next to the refrigerator there is a folder. Cheryl opens the folder and sees a large file. On the top of the first page she can see its divorce papers.

"What is this Gracie, some kind of a joke?" Cheryl asks as she begins to break down.

"It's no joke honey and Todd will be taking you to court for custody of the children." Gracie says with a sly voice as she hangs up in Cheryl's ear.

"Gracie, Gracie, you bitch." Cheryl says as she hangs up the phone in distraught.

"What's going on mom?" Danielle asks.

"Your father has decided to leave us. I'm guessing he took everything including all the money in the bank account too." Cheryl says in with tears pouring down her face.

Cheryl grabs onto Danielle and hugs her tight. She tries to hold back her emotions but she can't. It has been a long hard day and to come home and find everything gone, is a shock to the system.

"Where are we going to sleep tonight?" Michael asks as he walks into the kitchen.

"What do you mean, where are you going to sleep tonight." Cheryl says to Michael.

"All the beds are gone and my clothes are throw all over the floor. There is no furniture in the house." Michael replies.

Cheryl decides to take a walk around the house and see for herself. She is in shock to see all the furniture was moved out during the day while she was working. This whole thing was carefully planned out long before it was executed. Todd and his mother were working together and Cheryl knows it. The only things that remains in the house was everyone's clothes, with the exception of Todd's. Sad part about this scenario was the clothes were just thrown on the floor. Cheryl sits in a corner of her bedroom. She is in shock at what has just transpired. She and Todd worked so hard for what they had. She knows they were having a few problems but she figured they could work them out.

"Mom, I'm hungry. What's for dinner?" Michael asks.

"I don't know honey, let's go see what we have in the refrigerator." Cheryl says as she gets up and walks down the stairs with Michael.

Together they walk into the kitchen where Danielle is already standing. All the cupboards and the pantry door are wide open.

"Danielle, what are you doing?" Cheryl asks to her daughter that startles her.

"The son of a bitch took everything. There isn't even a morsel of food left in the house." Danielle replies.

"I don't want to hear that kind of language Danielle. Even though you did sum him up properly." Cheryl says as she opens the refrigerator.

Cheryl is shock to see Todd had even cleaned out the refrigerator. The house was completely wiped out. Cheryl is totally distraught and blinded sided. She has known Todd for over 14 years and this was totally unexpected. Cheryl opens her purse and sees she has twenty-two dollar in cash. She orders a cheese pizza and a two liter of Pepsi. After paying for the pizza, she only has three dollars and whatever change remaining in her purse. They sit in a circle on the living room floor and eat the pizza. There are no glasses, so they have to drink out of the two liter bottle. After they finish eating, Cheryl makes up a place to sleep on the master bedroom floor. They have to use their clothes for blankets because Todd took everything. By midnight both Danielle and Michael are sound asleep. Cheryl sits in the corner of her bedroom, and stares at her two children sleeping. Cheryl has tears in her eyes because she doesn't know what tomorrow is going to bring. Cheryl sits up most of the night thinking about what might have caused this. She runs different scenarios over and over in her head. She wants to know what she could have done wrong. Finally by three in the morning, Cheryl passes out from sheer exhaustion.

Chapter 3 – Saturday November 29th

The next morning, Cheryl is awakened by someone walking around downstairs. Cheryl quickly gets to her feet and walks towards the stairs. She can hear footsteps as the person went from room to room. Cheryl takes a look in the bedroom one last time and both kids are still sleeping. She closes the bedroom door and creeps down the stairway in her sock covered feet. When she reaches the landing she peeks around the corner. She waits a couple of minutes and then a strange man appears. He is tall and well dressed. Cheryl watches as he sets up a coffee table and a folding chair. He moves from room to room taking picture of the house. That is when Cheryl makes her move.

"What the hell do you think you're doing?" Cheryl says loudly and startles the man.

"I'm taking pictures of the house. It's going on the market December 1st." The man states.

"What? That can't be. The house is leased to us until March." Cheryl says.

"Are you Mrs. LaRussa?" The man asks.

"Yes I am." Cheryl answers with a confused voice.

"Well your husband broke the lease and your landlord Phil has decided to sell the house." The man says.

"This can't be. What is going on?" Cheryl says in despair.

"I'm sorry Mrs. LaRussa, I'm only doing my job." The man replies.

"The rent is paid through tomorrow, so get the hell out of here." Cheryl yells at the man.

"Yes ma'am." The man answers.

The real estate man packs up his belongings and leaves quickly. Cheryl reaches in her pocket and grabs out a few Advil for her oncoming headache. She goes into the refrigerator and takes out the two liter bottle of Pepsi. She pops the two Advil in her mouth and washes it down with the Pepsi as Michael walks in.

"What's for breakfast?" Michael asks.

"Cold pizza." Cheryl replies.

Michael grabs a piece of cold pizza and starts to eat it. Cheryl pulls out her cell phone and calls Phil the landlord. The phone rings once and he picks it up.

"Hello Phil Baker, how may I help you?" Phil says

"Phil, this is Cheryl LaRussa. What is going on?" Cheryl asks.

"Hi Cheryl, what do you mean by what's going on? Your husband told me you two bought a new house and you were moving out this weekend." Phil states.

"When did he say that?" Cheryl asks with concern.

"Shit, maybe back at the end of September." Phil answers.

"Phil, Todd left me and the kids. He took everything and I'm guessing he emptied the bank accounts too. The kids and I have nowhere to go." Cheryl pleads.

"I'm sorry Cheryl but the lease has been broken and I'm going to sell the house. I will give you until Monday morning to vacate the premises. You are paid through November and I will honor that." Phil answer.

"Phil, please we have nowhere to go." Cheryl asks politely.

"I'm sorry Cheryl, that's the best I can do." Phil says.

"How about the security deposit. Can you give that to me?" Cheryl asks.

"After I go through the house I will assess the damages and give you a check for the amount I think can be refunded. I will give you one piece of advice get yourself a good divorce lawyer." Phil says in a meaningful way.

"Thanks Phil, when can you assess the damages in the house? I have no money and nowhere to go." Cheryl says with tears streaming down her face.

"I'll stop by this afternoon." Phil says as he hangs up.

Cheryl hangs up the phone and realizes she has to get ready for work. She takes a quick shower and dresses business casual for the day. Wearing a green polo shirt and a pair of dress pants, she heads to work. She tells both Danielle and Michael to stay home and work on their school work. When Cheryl gets to work she punches in and goes to the customer service desk. She is busy all day directing patrons and answering questions. When she gets a free moment she checks her banking accounts. Cheryl can see Todd emptied both the checking and savings accounts. She is beside herself because they had over twenty thousand dollars in the savings account. That money she helped put there. They were going to use that money on a down payment for a new house. Being overwhelmed, Cheryl calls the bank to verify the account balances. The bank manager also tells Cheryl the accounts are closed. This only pisses Cheryl off even more knowing she got paid yesterday and he even took that. The day goes on and Cheryl is not her normal cheerful self. Then her boss and best friend arrives at work.

"Good morning Cheryl, how are you today?" Greta her boss asks.

Greta and Cheryl went to school together. They are best of friends and that goes back twenty years. Greta is a heavy set girl. She is also short at five feet two inches tall. She is not married, and lives in a two bedroom apartment by herself. She has brown hair cut into a bob. She wears glasses and loves to wear jewelry. Greta has a great personality and gets along with almost everyone with the exception of Todd. She told Cheryl not to marry him because he was no good.

"Not to good this morning Greta." Cheryl says with dejected voice.

"What's wrong honey?" Greta asks with concern.

"Todd left and took everything. I have no money and nowhere to live on Monday morning." Cheryl says as she starts to cry.

"That no good piece of crap. First of all you need to open you own bank account and then you need a good lawyer." Greta says as she takes Cheryl into the back room and away from the public.

Greta puts her arm around Cheryl as they walk into the back room to comfort her. Greta can see this ordeal has ripped a hole deep inside Cheryl's heart. Greta tells Cheryl to take the rest of the day off with pay. She gives Cheryl a piece of paper with a name and phone number on it.

"What this?" Cheryl asks.

"The name and number of a good lawyer." Greta says.

"Ryan DeCicero, why does that name sound so familiar?" Cheryl asks.

"He went to school us." Greta responds.

"He was the nerdy skinny guy. The one we use to call bookworm." Cheryl says.

"That's him," Greta replies as she hands Cheryl fifty dollars.

"What's that for?" Cheryl asks.

"You have kids to feed." Greta says with a smile

Cheryl gives Greta a hug and leaves work to go home. When she gets home she sees a check on the counter made out to her in the amount of one dollar. Even though the security deposit for one month's rent was nine hundred and twenty five dollars she would take that one dollar.

"This is bull shit, only one dollar back from our security deposit." Cheryl say

Cheryl runs to the bank to cash the check. She even opens up her own checking account. She hooks up direct deposit for her paycheck. On her way home Cheryl picks up some fast food for the kids and herself. When she gets home she stares at the piece of paper with Ryan DeCicero's number. Cheryl is fighting with herself to make the call. Even though it is Saturday most lawyers have an answering service. So Cheryl makes the call and leaves a message.

"Who did you call mom?" Danielle asks.

"A lawyer that Greta and I went to school with." Cheryl replies.

"Mom everything will work out." Danielle says to Cheryl as she gives her mom a hug.

"I know baby girl, I know." Cheryl replies as they hold each other tight.

The afternoon flies by and finally at four thirty in the afternoon Ryan calls Cheryl back. Cheryl goes over everything that happened and explains to Ryan that Todd took everything.

"You mean to say he cleaned out all the joint bank accounts?" Ryan asks.

"Yes and we have to be out of our house on Monday morning because Todd terminated the lease." Cheryl replies.

"Do you have anywhere to go?" Ryan asks.

"No, my parents have both passed away. I have no siblings or aunts and uncles. The only relative we have is Todd's mother and she won't do anything for me. She might take the kids in but that's all." Cheryl replies in a down and dejected voice.

Ryan takes the case knowing very well that Cheryl cannot pay for his services. He makes an appointment to meet with her on Sunday at her house. During the night they kept the same sleeping arrangements. Cheryl fell asleep immediately from sheer exhaustion. The initial shock was now behind her and the time for healing begins.

Chapter 4 – Lawyering Up

On Sunday morning, Cheryl gets up and takes a shower. The two children follow suite and they dress for church. Following the mass at St Anthony's, they attend the Sunday pancake breakfast. The breakfast is served to the family and friends of the parish that will help work on the Christmas festivities. These people volunteer their time to dress up the church for Christmas. Cheryl hardly ever volunteered her time to the church but now she needs faith more than ever. After mass, Cheryl kneels down in the pew and says a few more prayers. Over the past few years she has shied away from her faith. Cheryl knows she needs to be strong to get over this next bump in the road.

"Dear lord, I know I haven't believed in you as strongly as I did in the past. I know my faith has faded over the years. I have been a good mother and wife. I need your help now. Please make me strong and help me through this ordeal. I have nowhere else to turn. I'm all alone with two children to feed and no place to live. Please lord guide me in the right direction." Cheryl pleads in a prayer.

When Cheryl finishes her prayer, she and the kids go down to the basement of the church. The kids ask where they are going. Cheryl tells them they are volunteering to help the church during the Christmas season. Danielle is okay with it but Michael is putting up a stink about it. They make their way into the small kitchen and get in line for breakfast. Then Cheryl feels a tap on her shoulder and turns around to see Father Angelo.

"What have we here, Cheryl LaRussa? Where have you been my child? It has been years since you volunteered for our Christmas gala." Father Angelo says.

Father Angelo is short pudgy man with big round rosy cheeks. He is almost bald with just a little hair around his ears. Father Angelo has a big Italian nose with almond shaped eyes. He has been at St Anthony's for twenty-five years. He married Todd and Cheryl and baptized both children.

"Hi father, I know it's been a couple of years and I want to get the children involved." Cheryl replies.

"The more people we get involved the better I feel. This year we are looking for new ideas to dress up the church." Father Anthony says in a soft voice.

"I think the children and I would help immensely." Cheryl says with a smile.

"By the way, where is Todd?" Father Anthony asks.

"He decided to leave us father. I don't know where he is." Cheryl replies as she hold back her tears.

"Now, now my child everything will be alright. You have come to the right place." Father Anthony reassures her.

Cheryl and the children get their plates. They eat their breakfast and sit through the meeting. From there they go up into the church and begin decorating. At two in the afternoon Cheryl and children leave. She gets home and sees a strange man standing on the porch. Cheryl gets out of the car and confronts the man.

"Can I help you?" Cheryl asks.

"Hi Cheryl, its Ryan, Ryan DeCicero?" Ryan responds with a look of surprise.

"Ryan, I'm sorry you don't look like you did in high school." Cheryl says with a hand shake.

"Yeah, I changed a little over the years. No more tall skinny runt with zits." Ryan says laughingly.

Ryan standing six feet tall has broad shoulders and a well-built physic. He has a full head of dark brown hair that is parted on the side. He sports a thick bushy goatee. He is handsome and well mannered. He is dressed in a light blue button dress shirt with khaki pants. He is also wearing a pair of sneakers with a long trench coat that is unbuttoned.

"Come on in, I would ask you to take a seat but I have no furniture." Cheryl says.

"That's alright," Ryan replies.

The first thing Ryan wants to see is the divorce papers. Ryan leans against the counter in the kitchen and flips through the document. He reads quickly and flips page by page. Ryan is engrossed in the document as he reads it in silence for fifteen to twenty minutes.

"Is you husband a moron?" Ryan asks Cheryl.

"Why do you say that?" Cheryl replies.

"You're not signing this. He has everything incorporated in this document. If you signed it you would surrender full custody of the children to him. Let me take this with me so I can go through it with a fine tooth comb." Ryan says.

"Wow, I thought about just signing it and that would be the end of it." Cheryl says followed by a sigh.

"Good thing you didn't. When do you have to be out if here?" Ryan asks.

"Tomorrow," Cheryl responds disappointedly by putting her head down.

"Let me see what I can do. It may take a day or two." Ryan responds.

"Thank you so much." Cheryl says hopefully as she walks Ryan towards the door.

"What are you three having for dinner tonight?" Ryan asks.

"I don't know, I'm a little low on funds." Cheryl says.

"Come on, well go to Applebee's." Ryan says.

"I can't, we don't have much money." Cheryl responds.

"It's on me, get your coats and come on." Ryan answers with a smile from cheek to cheek.

"Come on mom, besides we're starving." Michael interrupts.

Cheryl laughs at Michael's response, besides it will give her a little time to catch up with an old classmate. They gather their coats and head out for dinner. They get a booth and place their orders for drinks. They all order soft drinks with the exception of Cheryl. She orders a water with lemon.

"So what have you been up to the past fourteen years?" Cheryl asks Ryan.

"Pre-law and law school ate up seven years. I worked for a firm for another five years. Then my dad got sick and I had to help my mom get him situated. I was with them for six months until I got them settled in assisted living down in Florida. When I got home, I opened my own practice. I specialize in divorce." Ryan says with a smile.

"Sorry to hear about your dad's illness." Cheryl replies.

"Thanks," Ryan responds.

They place their order for dinner with the waitress. Michael and Ryan talk about the football games being played on the televisions. Todd never once spent much time with his kids. He always sat in the recliner and slept after dinner.

"Did you ever get married?" Cheryl asks Ryan.

"No, I never found the right girl but I'm only thirty-four, I still have time." Ryan says with a smile.

Small talk continues during and after dinner. Both children get a dessert. They are giggling and having fun. When the check comes, Ryan pays for it. After that Ryan drives them back to the empty house.

"Thank you for everything." Cheryl says to Ryan with a handshake.

"It was my pleasure. I will call you sometime during the week and we can go over your case." Ryan replies.

"Okay and thanks again." Cheryl says as she closes his car door.

Cheryl walks towards the house and unlocks the front door. She and the kids make their way inside. They pack up all their clothes inside garbage bags. By nine pm both kids are sound asleep on the floor. Tomorrow school reopens after the five day Thanksgiving recess. Cheryl lays next to Danielle and looks at all the garbage bags filled with clothes spread across the floor. Three days ago she would have never imagined something like this. She thought Todd loved her but she guessed wrong. She looks around the room and reminisces about a house she called home for the past fourteen years. Tonight is the last night here. Tomorrow would be a different story because she has nowhere to go.

"We're being tossed out on the street. I just don't believe this." Cheryl says to herself as tears well in her eyes.

Cheryl starts crying knowing tomorrow they will probably be living in a shelter. How could Todd be so selfish and do this to his wife and children? The man really has no heart for his own kids. Cheryl puts her hand together and begins to pray again. She really has nowhere else to turn. She prays for what seems like hours or until she falls asleep.

Chapter 5 – Moving Day

The next morning, everyone gets up early to prepare for their day. Cheryl awakens first and gets into the shower. She gets dressed in her work clothes while Danielle and Michael get ready for school. There is nothing in the house to eat so they pack the trunk of the car with all their clothes.

"I'm hungry mom." Michael moans from the backseat of the car.

"Suck it up wimpy." Danielle yells to Michael sitting in the front seat.

"But I'm hungry. Listen you can hear my stomach grumbling." Michael yells back at Danielle as he rubs his stomach.

"Enough, the two of you. I have enough on my mind that I don't need to listen to you two argue." Cheryl says as she backs out of the driveway.

Cheryl backs out on the road and puts the car into drive. The three of them are looking at the house they called home for the past fourteen years. For Cheryl, this been home for the entire fourteen years she was married to Todd. For the children, this has been home for their entire lives. Cheryl turns her head forward and drives away. It's hard to leave and hold her tears back but she knows she has to stay strong for her children. Michael and Danielle look at the house until it goes out of sight. Cheryl drives to the middle school and drops Danielle off. She puts the car in park as Danielle opens the door.

"Here honey." Cheryl says as she rummages through her purse for a couple dollars.

"Mom, I can go without lunch." Danielle says.

"No, take the money." Cheryl demands.

Danielle takes the money and Cheryl watches her daughter walk into the school. She looks at her watch knowing Michael has a half an hour before he has to be at school.

"Okay hungry man, how about a breakfast sandwich from McDonalds?" Cheryl asks.

"Oh yeah, a bacon egg and sausage muffin would be good." Michael replies.

Cheryl takes Michael to McDonalds. She orders a breakfast sandwich for Michael and small coffee for herself. Cheryl gives Michael two dollars for lunch and drops him off at school. Michael opens the door to get out of the car.

"Where do I go after school?" Michael asks.

"Go to grandma's" Cheryl replies.

Cheryl heads to work and punches in one minute early. Today she works with the staff as they put up all the Christmas decorations throughout the store. This takes her mind off reality for a while because it brings back memories of her childhood. Back as a kid she would help her mother and father decorate the tree and the inside of their house. They even put lights outside the house and around the door.

"Hey Cheryl," Greta says pulling Cheryl back from the past and into the present.

"Huh, oh hi Greta." Cheryl replies with a startled voice.

"How are things going at home?" Greta asks.

"What home? Today I am officially homeless and broke with two mouths to feed." Cheryl says as she hangs a Christmas bulb from a ceiling tile.

"Like I told you, you and the kids can come and crash at my place." Greta responds with a smile.

"I can't do that to you. Let me see what Gracie says." Cheryl says with a grimace.

The work day goes by quickly. On her way out of work she checks her purse. She wants to see how much money she has and to her surprise, she only has about twenty-five dollars until pay day on Friday. Cheryl gets into her car and starts it up. She sits in despair as the low fuel light comes on.

"What did I do to deserve this? I was a loyal wife and a good mother. I work hard every day and I have nothing to my name." Cheryl says as she breaks down in the car.

Cheryl wipes her eyes and puts the car in drive as she pulls out of the parking lot. She drives over to Gracie's house to pick up the kids. She pulls into Gracie's driveway and gets out of the car. She walks up the steps leading to the porch. Cheryl softly knocks on the solid oak door. Gracie comes to the door and opens it.

"Hi mom are the kids here?" Cheryl asks in a soft kind voice.

"Yes, they're in the living room watching cartoons." Gracie responds as she lets Cheryl in the door.

Cheryl walks into the living room and sees Michael eating a bowl of cereal. Danielle is sitting on the couch doing her homework.

"Hi guys, how was school today?" Cheryl asks with a smile.

"Good," Michael replies with hype.

"Mom, we're putting on a Christmas play at school. I going to try out for the leading female part." Danielle replies.

"Wow, what's the play?" Cheryl asks with a smile.

"It's a Wonderful Life." Danielle replies.

"That's wonderful! Knock them dead honey." Cheryl says.

Cheryl walks into the kitchen and sits at the table with Gracie. Gracie is drinking a cup of coffee and smoking a cigarette. Cheryl is desperate and doesn't want to ask Gracie for help, but she has no alternative.

"Mom, can we stay here a few days until I get on my feet." Cheryl asks in a soft voice so the children don't hear her.

"First of all, since you're no longer married to my son please don't call me mom. Secondly, the children can stay until Friday and Friday only. Then you better have a place to stay or I'm throwing them out too." Gracie says loud and clear so the children can hear her.

"Thank you," Cheryl responds.

Cheryl doesn't have the guts to ask to borrow any money. Gracie is an old woman set in her ways. She likes her solitude and doesn't like anyone interrupting her lifestyle. Cheryl gathers up the children and they go out for dinner. She drives to the diner located on Main Street. The kids order a soft drink and she orders water. While kids order she adds the totals up in her head. Both meals and the sodas total nineteen dollars. The meals and tip will clean her out. Cheryl is a giving person and her needs come last. She watches as her children eat and she only drinks her water.

"Mom, aren't you going to order anything to eat?" Danielle asks.

"No I'm good, I ate something at work." Cheryl replies in a lie.

Danielle is a smart girl and knows her mother isn't eating because she doesn't have enough money to pay for it.

"I'm done, mom do you want to finish this?" Danielle asks as she pushes half of a hamburger and a hand full of fries in front of Cheryl.

Cheryl smiles at her daughter knowing they share the same behavior and personality. She slowly consumes the warm burger with the fries. Michael is oblivious to everything going on around him. When they finish dinner, Cheryl drives back to Gracie's house. She walks in with the children. Gracie is sitting in the living room watching her soap opera that is saved on her DVR. Cheryl acknowledges Gracie and brings the children upstairs to prepare them for bed. She tucks little Michael in bed and sits on the side of his bed. Cheryl reads him the story *"How the Grinch Stole Christmas."* Danielle lays on the adjoining twin bed doing her homework, but in reality she is listening to her mother read the story to Michael. As Cheryl finishes the book, she sees Michael is fast asleep. She kisses him on the forehead as she closes the book and puts it on the nightstand.

"Good night Danielle, sleep tight." Cheryl says as she leaves the bedroom.

Cheryl goes down stairs and sits in the living room with Gracie. Gracie is so infatuated with her soap operas and she doesn't even acknowledge Cheryl sitting on the sofa. When a commercial comes on she doesn't even fast forward it. That's when she turns to Cheryl with a cigarette dangling out of her mouth.

"So where are you sleeping tonight?" Gracie says with a stern voice.

This totally catches Cheryl off guard. She was expecting to sleep in the other spare bedroom.

"I, I'm sleeping at Greta's tonight." Cheryl stutters and lies.

"Then you better get going because I'm locking the door and going to bed in a few minutes." Gracie replies.

Cheryl grabs her coat and purse and heads out the door. She is lucky because tonight the temperature is only going down to forty-five degrees. Cheryl knows she is low on gas so if she sleeps in the car she won't be able to start the car to warm up. She passes by Greta's apartment and knocks on the door. There is no answer so Cheryl leaves. She drives downtown and parks her car in the parking lot at the store where she works. She turns off the car and locks the doors. Cheryl climbs in the backseat and cuddles up with the kids sweat jackets. There she cries herself to sleep.

Chapter 6 – Tuesday December 2nd

On Tuesday morning, Cheryl is awakened by someone knocking on her car window. The sound startles her as she looks up and sees a police officer. Cheryl climbs over to the front seat and rolls the window down just a crack.

"Yes officer?" Cheryl says in a sleepy voice.

"The night manager called us. He said someone was loitering in the parking lot." Officer Jefferson says.

"No sir, I work here. I got here too early for work so I decided to take a nap." Cheryl replies to cover herself.

"Ma'am, have you been drinking?" Officer Jefferson asks.

"No sir," Cheryl replies.

"Please get out of the car with your license and registration." Officer Jefferson says in a stern voice.

Cheryl looks out the window and notices it's still dark out. She slowly rolls the window up. She reaches in her purse and gets her license and registration and gets out of the car. Cheryl is exhausted and cold from the elements. Officer Jefferson shines his flashlight on her license and looks at Cheryl to make sure she is the person on license. Then Officer Jefferson pulls out a breathalyzer and instructs Cheryl to blow into it.

"Officer, I have not been drinking." Cheryl states in a confident voice.

"We shall see about that. No one just parks in a parking and sleeps unless they have had to much the drink." Officer Jefferson says as he puts the tube up to her mouth.

Cheryl knows she is not drunk so she blows into the breathalyzer to appease the police officer. The officer looks at the dial of the breathalyzer and waits for the results. Cheryl stands there with her hands in her pockets freezing.

"Okay, I guess you were telling the truth about drinking. Now tell me why you are sleeping in your car in your employer's parking lot?" Officer Jefferson demands.

Cheryl turns away with tears in her eyes again. She breaks down and has a hard time answering officer Jefferson.

"I have nowhere to live and no money." Cheryl says with tears streaming down her face.

"I though you said you work here?" Officer Jefferson questions her.

"I do work here. My husband left me and took everything. I have a total of thirty-three cents to my name and that's all I have left to make it till Friday when I get paid." Cheryl says as she wipes her tears on the sleeve of her coat.

"Wow, I am really sorry miss but we need to go inside to verify that you work here. This way I don't have to take you in for loitering." Officer Jefferson says.

Cheryl and Officer Jefferson walk across the parking lot towards the front door of the grocery store. Officer Jefferson is a thirty-one year old black male. He has been on the police force for ten years. In high school, he was all state linebacker that was drafted by the Michigan State. He destroyed his shoulder in his freshman year and that was the end of his football career. Officer Jefferson stands six feet three inches tall and weighs around two hundred and forty pounds. His hair is cut short with no facial hair. He is a professional police officer and takes his job seriously. When they arrive at the front door, the night manager is waiting. He recognizes Cheryl face as she walks through the door.

"Cheryl, what are you doing sleeping in the parking lot?" Ricky the night manager asks.

"It's a long story." Cheryl says sheepishly as she can't look Ricky in the eyes.

"Thank you officer, I can take it from here." Ricky tells Officer Jefferson.

"Cheryl, everything will work out." Officer Jefferson says as he walks out of the store.

Ricky brings Cheryl into his office. He grabs a couple of cups of coffee and two donuts. Cheryl eats the donut like a hungry kid that hasn't eaten in days. They sit down and Cheryl goes through the entire story telling Ricky everything. Again she breaks down and continuously wipes the tears off her face with her jacket sleeve. Ricky sits there in amazement at what has transpired in this girl's life in just five days. Ricky is a young night manager at the age of twenty-five. He stands five feet nine inches tall with a medium build. He has long blonde hair pulled back into a ponytail. He is a handsome kid with a blonde reddish mustache. He started working for the large grocery chain as a night stocker. He worked his way up into management because of eagerness to give one hundred and ten percent every day. He cares about himself, his employees, the customers and most of all his employer.

"What time do you have to be at work today?" Ricky asks.

"Nine." Cheryl replies.

Cheryl looks at the clock and sees it's almost seven.

"I have to go. I have to get the kids to school." Cheryl says as she walks towards the door.

"Here take this and get something to eat. This is all I have." Ricky says as he pulls the contents out of his wallet.

"I can't take your money." Cheryl pleads as pushes the money back to Ricky.

"Listen, call it a loan. You have two kids you need to feed. I have just me. Take the money, I will survive." Ricky says as he gives her two hundred and twenty-two dollars.

Cheryl takes the money and thanks Ricky with a kiss on the cheek. She runs out to the car and drives to Gracie's house to pick up the kids. When she gets there they are waiting outside on the porch. They get into the car. Her first stop is the gas station to put in twenty dollars in gas.

"Did you guys eat yet?" Cheryl asks the kids.

"No grandma was still sleeping when we left. We didn't want to disturb her." Danielle says.

"I'm hungry!" Michael moans from the backseat.

Cheryl takes the kids to a diner. They order breakfast and all three of them clean their plates. Cheryl drives the kids to school. She stops over at Greta's house and takes a shower. She dresses for work and arrives just in the nick of time. She punches in and works with the crew putting up Christmas decorations again. Another day of work that keeps her mind off what is happening in her personal life. Then her cell phone starts to ring. She looks at the number and notices its Ryan.

"Hello!" Cheryl says.

"Hi Cheryl, its Ryan. I just got off the phone with Todd's lawyer. Boy was he surprised to find out you have a lawyer. I think they were guessing you were going to just sign the divorce papers and that would be the end of it." Ryan says with enthusiasm.

"I don't know how to thank you." Cheryl says with a smile.

"Don't worry about that right now. I have more news. We are going to bring this in front of a judge. Wait until he sees these divorce papers he is going to go through the roof. I think Todd's lawyer is starting to sweat" Ryan says eagerly.

"Wow, thank you so much." Cheryl exclaims with sincerity.

"I'm not done yet. I have a friend whose parents own a house out by the lake. His parents live in Florida from November through April. The house is sitting vacant and it's completely furnished. He called them and explained to them about your situation, and do you know what they told him." Ryan says.

"I don't know. What did they say?" Cheryl says with her fingers crossed.

"They said by all means, have her move in right away." Ryan says with happiness.

"Oh my god, thank you." Cheryl says aloud in the store.

"I am so happy I could help. By the way I will have the keys to the house tomorrow." Ryan says.

"Hey would you like to help us move in? I will make dinner." Cheryl says.

"I don't know that depends what you're making for dinner. Of course I'll help you guys move in." Ryan says.

Ryan hangs up and Cheryl continues to work. She has a brighter smile and a spring in her step. That's until she hears her name called over the PA system. The voice sounds like Mr. Robbins, the store manager. Cheryl walks towards the front of the store where the manager's office is located. She is nervous and doesn't know what to expect. When she reaches the store managers' office, she knocks on the door.

"Come in," Mr. Robbins says.

Cheryl walks in and her mouth is dry because she doesn't know what this is about. She has always been a good employee. She is never late and only called in sick once in three years. As she walks in to her surprise he is not alone. There is another man there dressed in a suit.

"Hi Cheryl, come on in and take a seat." Mr. Robbins says.

"Hello Mr. Robbins." Cheryl says as she walks into his office.

James Robbins has been the store manager for the last ten years. He is a big heavy man with a round pot belly. He is bald and always dresses up for work in a suit and tie. Mr. Robbins is always walking through the store. He always says hello to all the employees and patrons. He may be a hard ass when it comes to work but he is always fair.

Cheryl walks in and takes a seat in front of his desk. She sits with her legs straight down and both arms nervously glued down to the arms of the chair. Cheryl thinks hard at what she might have done wrong to land in the manager's office.

"Cheryl, I would like to introduce you to Stephen Boyd. He is the owner of Boyd's Supermarkets." Mr. Robbins says to Cheryl.

"Hi Mr. Boyd, it's a pleasure to meet you." Cheryl says as she shakes his hand.

"Hi Cheryl, the pleasure is all mine." Stephen replies.

"You're probably wondering why you were called down here?" Mr. Robbins asks.

"Yes I am," Cheryl answers with caution in her voice.

"Well it been brought to my attention that your spouse has left you homeless and broke. Is that true?" Mr. Robbins states.

"Yes it is," Cheryl says sheepishly as she nods her head up and down.

"Well we're going to help you in every way we can. You have been a loyal employee with a great work record and we're not going to let you live out on the street." Mr. Robbins says with a stern straight forward voice.

"My lawyer just found me and the kids a place to live for a couple of months." Cheryl replies.

"Okay, how about food and money to live off?" Mr. Robbins asks.

"I just have the money that Ricky, the night manager, loaned me. It will get me through a couple of days" Cheryl says.

"To show we are family here at Boyd's, here is a one thousand dollar Boyd's gift card and five hundred dollars cash." Stephen Boyd says as he hands her an envelope.

"I can't take this." Cheryl pleads.

"It's a gift from us to you. Merry Christmas to you and your family." Stephen says.

Cheryl starts to gets emotional with tears running down her face. She thanks her managers again and finishes her day at work. Cheryl picks up her kids and they get something to eat. Then they spend the night in a hotel. She tells the children about her day and about the house on the lake. The kids get excited about the house. By ten in the evening the kids go to sleep while Cheryl takes a long hot shower. She gets out of the shower and cuddles up on the bed. She smiles as she looks over at her two children sleeping so sound.

"Thank you," Cheryl says looking up at the ceiling with her hands folded together like she is praying

Chapter 7 – The House on the Lake

On Wednesday morning December 3rd, the children went to school and Cheryl is only working a half day because she was meeting Ryan. He was bringing her the keys to the house. Today Cheryl is working at the customer service desk. The hustle and bustle of the holidays is now in full gear. People moving through the store getting Christmas gifts and groceries. At twelve fifty-five pm, Cheryl is taking care of her last customer when Ryan arrives at the store. Her final customer is an old man cashing in his scratch off lottery ticket. Ryan waves and stands off to the side while Cheryl tends to her customer. Cheryl takes the ticket and scans it.

"Twenty dollar winner, nice!" Cheryl says to the man as she hands him the twenty dollar bill.

"Hey, every once in while you get lucky in life." The old man replies.

The old man is dressed in rags and his thin coat is dirty with a few rips in it. His hair is uncombed with a scruffy un-groomed beard. He smells like he hasn't bathed in months. Cheryl looks into his bloodshot eyes and sees a man that has lived a hard life. When she touches his hand to place the bill in, she can feel the calluses and dried skin. Cheryl looks at the old man and sympathizes with his life. She knows he is worse off than her. Then Cheryl remembers there is an old coat of Todd's sitting in the trunk of her car.

"Thank you," The old man says as he puts the twenty dollar bill in his pocket.

"You're welcome, sir. Hey, wait a minute I have an old coat of my husbands in my car. It's not brand new but it will be a lot warmer than the one you are wearing." Cheryl says as she lifts the counter up and exits from behind the customer service desk.

"You don't have to do that for me." The old man says with pride.

"Yes I do. The coat is my ex-husbands and it's such a nice coat it would be a shame to let it go to waste. I'm getting out of work now. Let me get my things and I will get the coat out of my car for you." Cheryl says with a smile.

Cheryl walks over to the time clock and punches out for the day. She goes into the backroom and gets her coat and purse out of her locker. She knows it's been hard for her over the past couple days and this man has a lot less than she does. Cheryl is so thankful for what her managers and Ryan have done for her. Things could be a lot worse and she and kids could be living out on the street. When she returns to the front of the store Ryan is talking to the old man.

"Come on lets go." Cheryl says as they walk out into the cold weather.

The old man has a hard time walking. His joints are full with arthritis from years of working and living out in the elements. When they reach the car, Cheryl unlocks the trunk with the key. She digs through the bags of clothing until she finds the old heavy parka. She pulls the coat out of the bag and gives it to the old man. He quickly puts the coat over his old one. Another layer will help keep him warm during the cold winter nights.

"Thank you for your generosity. I know you are a good person and there are brighter days ahead. Don't let your husband's unfaithful ways keep you away from your faith." The old man says as he walks away.

"What did you tell him about my husband?" Cheryl asks Ryan.

"Absolutely nothing." Ryan replies with surprise.

"Then what were you two talking about when I came up front?" Cheryl asks.

"He was telling me about how people don't have faith any more. The belief of Jesus is no longer part of Christmas. It's all about the commercialized buying of gifts." Ryan replies.

"Really, but I wonder how he knows about me and my husband?" Cheryl says as she and Ryan looks towards the old man.

"Where is he?" Ryan asks Cheryl with surprise.

Both Cheryl and Ryan look in the direction the man was walking in and he is gone.

"He should be right there. He doesn't walk very fast." Cheryl replies.

"Maybe he ducked out of sight." Ryan says as they look in between the parked cars.

They look around for five minutes and figure the man was picked up by a car or bus. There were no sirens so he wasn't injured.

"Come on, let's go to the house. He is alright." Ryan states as they get into separate cars and drive to the house.

They drive three miles until they reach the side of the lake. Cheryl is following Ryan as they drive down West Lake Road. They drive about two more miles and Ryan turns up a driveway. It's a long and winding driveway with many trees covering the house. The driveway is about six hundred feet long. When the house comes in view Cheryl is in awe. The two story house is only a couple of years old. The white house is up on the hillside. It faces towards the lake with many bay windows. The house has a wraparound porch with a double swing chair facing the lake. They both get out of their cars and meet on the bottom step of the porch.

"Wow! It's a beautiful house. What did your friends parents do for a living?" Cheryl asks in awe of the immaculate home in front of her.

"His father was lawyer and his mother was a homemaker and they retired a few years ago. They found this spot and built their dream home to retire in." Ryan says with a smile.

"Then why aren't they here? It so beautiful." Cheryl says as she walks up the steps.

"The father is sick and the mother is taking care of him. The cold weather bothers him and he is in constant pain. That is why they go to Florida for the cold winter months." Ryan says as he puts the key into the lock.

When they walk into the house, Cheryl is amazed of the beautiful oak wood trim. The foyer leads into to a great room with a large wood burning fireplace. The fireplace is made of red brick with a sandstone mantle and base. The great room has a cathedral ceiling with large wooden beams decorating the ceiling. The great room is furnished with two plush couches facing the fire place. One couch to the left, and one to the right with a 55 inch plasma TV located over the top of the fire place. Then Cheryl walks into the large Italian style kitchen with all stainless steel appliances. There is large island with a pot rack hanging over the top of it. The wooden kitchen cabinets are made of dark cherry wood. The kitchen has recessed lighting that adds to the aura of the home. The dining room is located off the kitchen and has a large oak table with eight place settings. To the back of the kitchen there is a small mud room with a brand new washer and dryer.

"This is unbelievable, why would your friends parents let us stay here?" Cheryl asks.

"First of all, they hate to leave this house unattended. Someone could break in and steal all the contents. With someone living here a break in is highly unlikely." Ryan answers.

They head back to the front of the house and walk up the wrapping oak staircase that leads to the second floor. The second floor has two bedrooms, a master bedroom, an office, and two bathrooms including the master bath. All the bedrooms have queen size beds and are fully furnished with dressers, night stands, TVs and a dressing chair.

"Oh my god this is beautiful!" Cheryl says with her hands over her cheeks.

"Come on let's get the clothes out of your trunk." Ryan says.

Cheryl and Ryan get the clothes and put them away in the bedrooms. When they look at the clock and Cheryl realizes she needs to pick up the kids from school. They both jump into Ryan's car and get Danielle first.

"What does the house look like?" Danielle asks eagerly as she gets into Ryan's car.

"Let's put it this way Danielle, you are going to be amazed when you see the living space and your bedroom. Remember, this is only temporary." Cheryl replies with a smile.

"Anything is better than grandma's house and hotel rooms. "Danielle says.

They leave the middle school and go pick up Michael before they head to the grocery store.

"Why are we at Boyd's?" Michael asks.

"You want to eat buddy?" Cheryl replies to her son.

"Yes," Michael says

"Then we need food." Cheryl replies.

All four of them go shopping together. They buy meat, produce, canned goods, dry goods, frozen food and munchies. Cheryl uses up over five hundred dollars from her gift card. They load up Ryan's trunk with little space remaining. When they pull out of the parking lot Cheryl notices the old man sitting on a park bench. He waves and smiles at Cheryl as they pull out of the parking lot. Cheryl waves back while the old man points to the coat and gives her a thumbs up sign. Cheryl smiles back at the old man as he takes a sip from a foam cup. He is drinking coffee and eating a donut while watching the cars drive by.

"It looks like the old man likes the coat I gave him." Cheryl says to Ryan.

"How do you know that?" Ryan asks.

"He is sitting on the park bench across from Boyd's parking lot. He smiled at me and gave me a thumbs up." Cheryl replies.

"Really, I didn't see him." Ryan states.

"How could you miss him your head lights were shining on him as you turned out of the parking lot?" Cheryl says with concern.

"I wasn't paying attention to the park bench, I was looking at the road." Ryan responds.

They go back to the house and put the groceries away. Cheryl cooks up a four burgers on the inside grill with a side salad and a vegetable. After dinner, the four of them sit in the great room watching *The Polar Express*.

"We need to put up a Christmas tree and get some wood for the fireplace." Danielle says.

"Sounds like a plan for tomorrow night." Cheryl says as she gives Danielle a hug.

After the movie Ryan heads home. Cheryl gives him a hug and thanks him for all the help he has provided them. By ten o'clock both kids are in bed and sound asleep. Cheryl finishes cleaning the kitchen and wants to relax a little bit. She puts on her pajamas and robe and goes back downstairs. She sits on the couch sipping a mug of hot chocolate.

"I don't know if you had anything to do with this, but I thank you with all my heart." Cheryl says while looking up to the heavens.

Chapter 8 – The Christmas Tree

On Thursday morning December 4th, Cheryl makes the kids pancakes and sausage for breakfast. They are off to school and work after the breakfast dishes are done. Cheryl drops the children off at school before she heads to work. As she turns into the parking lot, Cheryl looks at the vacant park bench. She knows she saw the old man sitting there last night. Maybe Ryan really wasn't paying attention. The work day is the same as usual during the holiday season. The days go by fast and soon its lunch time. Cheryl didn't bring anything so she grabs a sub and a coffee right in the store. Then she sees the old man walk into the store. He is wearing Todd's old jacket as Cheryl makes eye contact. The old man waddles his way over to Cheryl's table.

"Would you like to join me? I bought a whole sub and that's too much for me." Cheryl says to the old man.

"I don't mind if I do." The old man replies.

Cheryl gives the old man the other half of her turkey sub. She buys him a large coffee as they sit and talk about the holidays. The old man is very knowledgeable about Christmas and shares that with Cheryl. The half hour lunch goes buy fast and Cheryl realizes she has to get back to work.

"By the way what is your name?" Cheryl asks.

"You know who I am." The old man replies with a smile.

Cheryl turns around to walk to the time clock. She turns around to say something to the old man and he is not there. She looks towards the exit and sees a glimpse of the blue coat leaving the store. Cheryl thinks nothing of it as she goes back to work. She figures he is suffering from the beginning stages of dementia. The day goes by fast and soon her shift is over. Cheryl drives to the middle school and picks up Danielle. They drive over to the elementary school and wait for Michael. Cheryl uses her iPhone and finds a supplier of cut wood. She calls and orders two cords of wood to be delivered at her new address. As soon as she hangs up the phone, Ryan calls in.

"Hello," Cheryl says.

"Hi Cheryl, I have good news. The court date is set for Tuesday December 16th at 10 am." Ryan says with enthusiasm.

"The only thing I want out of this is full custody of the children. He doesn't deserve to even get joint custody. He never did anything with the kids." Cheryl says with sincerity.

"Cheryl he doesn't have a leg to stand on. Especially with what he did to you and the children, leaving you homeless and penniless." Ryan states.

"Good, I hope the judge hammers him." Cheryl says.

"I have been putting together a solid case against Todd. I have a private investigator working for me, and I have some bad news and it's hard to explain." Ryan says.

"What did Todd do?" Cheryl asks with her voice breaking.

"Your ex-husband Todd has knocked up one of the office girls at the dealership that he worked at. They both quit working there and moved out of state. From what I heard he is somewhere in Arizona. They are shacked up together and he is selling cars down there." Ryan says.

"That bastard! I had a feeling something was wrong. I hope he rots in hell for what he put us through." Cheryl says with tears welling in her eyes.

"I know it's hard, but I'm going to make this right for you. We're going after child support and health insurance." Ryan says.

Cheryl wipes the tears from her eyes. Todd just pushed the dagger deeper into her back. Cheryl does her best to hold back her emotions.

"Ryan, you do what you have to. Take him to the bank. Let's hit him where it hurts." Cheryl says.

"I plan on it." Ryan responds.

As they hang up, Cheryl tells Danielle of the news about her father. Danielle doesn't take it well as she begins to cry. Cheryl grabs a hold of Danielle and holds her tight. She reassures her that she will never leave her or Michael. Her love is too deep for her children and they are her life. Cheryl can't imagine life without her children.

"Where is he?" Danielle asks.

"He is somewhere in Arizona." Cheryl says as she looks out the window and wipes the tears from her eyes.

"That's a far cry from home here in central New York." Danielle says as she sees Michael running towards the car.

"I guess he needed to get as far away as he could." Cheryl says as Michael gets into the car.

They make their way home and Cheryl prepares a pasta dinner. After dinner they go out and get a real Christmas tree. They bring the tree home and place it on the front porch.

"Okay we need to buy some decorations and lights for the tree." Cheryl says to the kids.

"Why? There is a tree stand and boxes of lights and decorations in the basement." Michael says.

"What, how do you know that?" Cheryl asks with a look of concern on her face.

"I went exploring yesterday when you were cooking." Michael says with a smile.

"What else did you do while I was cooking?" Cheryl asks.

"Well the tub in your bathroom has a Jacuzzi." Michael replies with a smile on his face.

"Alright enough with your findings. Let's get inside and get those decorations from the basement and put that tree up." Cheryl says with an upbeat voice.

The three of them go inside and the kids bring up all the Christmas decorations from the basement. Cheryl makes some hot chocolate and brings the mugs into the great room. It takes all three of them to set the tree into the stand. Danielle decides to turn on the stereo. She tunes into a station playing Christmas carols. The three of them have so much fun putting up the tree. This is the first time they really spent time together as a family. They have grown closer to each other more than they ever have been in the past.

"We'll be rocking around, the Christmas tree its Christmas party hop." Cheryl says as she starts to sing along with the radio.

Danielle joins in and Michael plays along because he doesn't know lyrics to the song. They dance around the tree while putting on the lights. Then, the garland and bulbs follow until the tree is fully decorated.

"What's this?" Michael says as he show Cheryl a couple of packages of tinsel.

"Its tinsel, you hang it off the tree branches." Cheryl replies.

"Can we put it on the tree?" Michael asks with enthusiasm.

"I don't see why not." Cheryl replies.

Both Danielle and Michael get the tinsel out of the packages and start hanging the silver strands. Cheryl sits back on the sofa and admires the beautiful tree sitting in the middle of the great room. Then there is a knock on the door. Cheryl goes to the door and answers it. It's the wood man and he has the wood for the fireplace. He asks Cheryl where to put the wood and she instructs him to put the wood on the front porch for easy access. Cheryl pays the man and he and his son unload the wood. Cheryl returns to the couch and sits. She grabs her mug of hot chocolate and she takes a sip.

"Should I?" Michael mouth the words to Danielle.

Danielle nods her head yes. Michael drapes tinsel on top of Cheryl's auburn hair. The tinsel dangles over Cheryl's eyes.

"Alright wise guy." Cheryl says as she gets up and chases Michael around the house.

Michael runs into the kitchen and Cheryl follows him. He runs into the dining room and around the table. Cheryl follows closely as she cuts the distance between her and her son. Then she tackles him in the foyer and drags him by his feet into the great room. There she sets him on the floor and begins to tickle him under his arm pits. Michael laughs out hysterically while Cheryl uses her fingers.

"Stop it, stop it your killing me." Michael yells out in between laughing.

"What's the matter big boy? Can't take the pain of the ticklers." Cheryl says as she continues to tickle Michael.

Danielle joins in with Cheryl and helps her tickle Michael. He giggles and screams out hysterically into the night.

"Okay I give up, I give up." Michael says as he tries to roll away.

"Are you sure you give up?" Cheryl asks.

"Yes, yes, yes." Michael answers.

They finish playing around. They turn off all the lights and admire the lights on the Christmas tree.

"Wow, mom the tree is absolutely beautiful." Danielle says.

"Yes it is," Cheryl replies.

"I don't see anything great about it." Michael states.

"I think you're asking for the ticklers again." Danielle says to Michael.

"Oh no more ticklers. The tree looks great." Michael says.

"Mom, there is only one thing that could make this a memorable night?" Danielle asks.

"What's that honey?" Cheryl asks.

"A fire in the fireplace." Danielle replies.

"Yes, I think you right!" Cheryl answers.

They go outside and grab five logs with some kindling. Cheryl opens the flue and starts the fire. She throws three of the logs on the fire. The three of them sit on the couch and listen to the Christmas carols with the fire burning brightly. Cheryl admires the tree with the LED lights. One by one the children fall asleep on the couch. Michael is first and about thirty minutes later Danielle follows. Cheryl carries Michael up to his bedroom while Danielle staggers up behind them. Cheryl tucks Michael under the covers and turns off his light. She goes over to Danielle's room as she gets into her bed.

"Good night honey." Cheryl says to Danielle as she turns off her light.

"Good night mom." Danielle says under her breathe.

Cheryl goes back downstairs and gets herself a glass of red wine. She enjoys the rest of the evening while the fire burns. She counts her blessings and thanks God she has two healthy children. They have a temporary roof over their heads with plenty of food in the pantry. Cheryl realizes things could have been a lot worse. As she takes a sip of wine she pulls her ponytail out. She turns her head from side to side to loosen up her hair over her shoulders. Cheryl pulls up a small afghan as she relaxes to the music. She get comfortable with the pillows as she stares into the fire. Within fifteen to twenty minutes, Cheryl passes out. The fire slowly burns out and Cheryl is snoring away with the Christmas carols playing softly in the background.

Chapter 9 – Friday December 5th

The next morning, Cheryl is awakened by the coldness in the house. The draft is coming from the fireplace. She sees the fire has burned out and she didn't close the two glass doors. Cheryl looks at her watch and sees it's almost six in the morning. She gets up off the couch closes the fireplace doors, turns off the music and Christmas tree lights. Cheryl puts the empty wine glass in the kitchen and then goes upstairs to shower. The warm water feels good flowing over her body. She remembers today is pay day and this time Todd cannot steal her money. Cheryl knows she needs to buy a few Christmas gifts for the kids. Her money is limited and so are the Christmas gifts. A little something is better than nothing. She gets dressed, takes the kids to school and goes to work. Cheryl gets out of work at three pm and as she walking to her car her cell phone rings. She looks at the screen and sees its Todd.

"What do you want?" Cheryl says loudly.

"Hey, I'm calling to see how the kids are?" Todd asks

"If you were here you would know how the kids are." Cheryl snaps back.

"I'm sorry for what I did but it's for the best." Todd says.

"You don't know the meaning of sorry." Cheryl replies sarcasm.

"What is this? You have a lawyer and you're not going to sign the divorce papers?" Todd asks.

"You're crazy if you think I'm giving you full custody of our children." Cheryl replies with anger.

"What are you talking about?" Todd asks like he is concerned.

"You know dam well what I'm talking about. The clause in the divorce papers stating I'm surrendering custody of the kids to you." Cheryl yells as she unlocks her car and gets in.

"Oh," Todd replies.

"You must really think I'm stupid. You know what, I shouldn't be talking to you anyway." Cheryl says as she hangs up on him.

Cheryl goes and gets the kids and brings them home. She throws a chicken with vegetables into the oven. She sets the timer for an hour and a half. She leaves the kids home to do their homework. Cheryl makes her way down the mall to purchase a few gifts for the kids. She knows she can't afford to buy them what they want. She gets Michael a New York Yankee's cap and some coloring books. She gets Danielle some hair accessories and a new blouse. This depletes her seventy dollars that she set aside from this week's pay check. On her way home she receives a call from Ryan. He wants to know if she will be home tonight because he wants to go over her case. Cheryl invites Ryan over for dinner as she heads home. When she gets home the timer on the stove has seven minutes remaining. The house has the aroma of home cooked chicken flowing throughout. Cheryl goes upstairs and puts the gifts in her bedroom closet. She runs a brush through her hair as the doorbell rings.

"Danielle, get the door, I'll be right down." Cheryl yells from the master bath.

Cheryl makes her way downstairs and Ryan is standing in the foyer. He has a paper bag in his right hand and folder in his left hand. Then the oven timer starts beeping.

"Come on in and make yourself comfortable." Cheryl says as she goes into the kitchen.

"I brought some wine for dinner." Ryan replies as he follows her into the kitchen.

"The wine opener and glasses are right over there." Cheryl says to Ryan as she points towards the small mini bar located at the end of the counter top.

Cheryl takes the chicken and vegetable out of the oven. Ryan opens the bottle of wine and pours two glasses. Cheryl calls the children to dinner as they grab their plates. Cheryl grabs her plate followed by Ryan. They sit at the dining room table and begin to eat. Ryan doesn't get many home cooked meals being single and working all kinds of crazy hours.

"What kind of chicken is this?" Ryan asks.

"Good chicken," Michael replies.

"Baked chicken with vegetables." Cheryl replies.

"Yeah but the chicken just melts in your mouth." Ryan says while devours the food on his plate.

"That's because I cooked it in my Dutch oven." Cheryl says with a smile.

"What kind of seasoning did you use?" Ryan asks as he takes a second helping out of the Dutch oven and puts it onto his plate.

"Salt, pepper and Italian seasonings." Cheryl says as she breaks the chicken apart on her plate.

"So not only are you a working mom but you're a good cook too." Ryan replies.

Cheryl smiles at the pleasant remark because Todd never complimented her. When dinner is done Danielle cleans off the table and loads the dishwasher. Ryan and Cheryl sit at the table with their wine while he goes over her case. He explains to Cheryl that she has a ninety-nine percent chance to keep full custody of the children. In addition she should receive an ample amount child support from Todd.

"Speaking of Todd, he called me today!" Cheryl says with concern.

"What did he want?" Ryan asks.

"He wanted to know how the kids were doing and why I haven't signed the divorce papers." Cheryl replies.

"What did you tell him?" Ryan asks.

"That he wasn't going to get full custody of the children and that's why I didn't sign the paper." Cheryl says.

"He is just feeling you out for answers. Next time he calls don't even answer it." Ryan responds.

They finish going over the paperwork and Ryan takes them out to Friendly's for an ice cream. Michael gets a hot fudge sundae and Danielle gets a caramel sundae. Cheryl and Ryan share a Jim Dandy.

"Oh by the way, what do I owe your friends parents for the rent?" Cheryl asks as she grabs for her checkbook.

'Nothing, they don't want anything. They just want to help. All's they ask in return is to make sure everything is left the way you found it." Ryan says.

"I can't do that but I have to pay something" Cheryl replies.

"They said no, they want to help." Ryan insists.

After dessert Ryan drives them home. He tells Cheryl that he will call her over the weekend after he finishes up more details in her case. Cheryl and kids thank him for dessert as Ryan backs his car down the driveway. Cheryl and the kids walk towards the house as a light snow begins to fall. Cheryl and kids stand out in the snow shower. They admire the glistening snowflakes as the shimmer from the street lights.

"Maybe we'll have a white Christmas." Michael says as he catches snowflakes on his tongue.

"Maybe, we still have three weeks until Christmas." Cheryl replies.

They sit out in the light snow for a few minutes. Then they go into the house for the night. The temperature outside is around thirty degrees. The snow squalls will melt in the morning when the temperature goes up to forty. When they get inside the house they relax on the couch while watching reruns of *The Big Bang Theory*. Cheryl laughs out loud and enjoys the comedy as she has another glass of wine while the kids have a cup of hot chocolate. Then Cheryl remembers she has to work for four hours in the morning. She picks up her cell phone and calls her mother-in-law Gracie.

"Hello," Gracie says.

"Hi Gracie it Cheryl. I was calling to ask if you wouldn't mind watching the kids for a couple of hour's tomorrow morning while I work." Cheryl asks.

"I can't I have an appointment tomorrow." Gracie replies with attitude.

"Tomorrow is Saturday, what appointment do you have on a Saturday?" Cheryl asks with concern.

"I have a hair appointment." Gracie replies rudely.

"I'm sorry for inconveniencing you. Goodbye." Cheryl say as she hangs up in disgust.

"Mom we don't need a babysitter. I can watch Michael for the few hours while you're working. Besides I have a school project I have to work on" Danielle says.

"I'm alright with it, just don't answer the door or let anyone in the house." Cheryl responds.

Danielle agrees with her mother and tries to help out where she can. By ten pm the entire family is in bed sleeping. A long and trying day finally comes to an end.

Chapter 10 – The Accident

The next morning, Cheryl gets up at six in the morning. She is working from seven to eleven. She takes her shower and dresses for work. Before she leaves the house for work, she checks in on the kids. She looks in each bedroom and sees they are still sleeping. She knows she will have an hour or two in at work before they get up. She arrives at work on time and punches in. Cheryl gets behind the customer service counter and notices Greta is working with her.

"I thought you were off today?" Cheryl asks Greta.

"I was off until Roberta called in sick." Greta replies.

"Hey are you going to the company Christmas party next Saturday?" Greta asks.

"I don't know, I don't have anyone to watch the kids." Cheryl replies.

"It's always a fun night with free booze and dancing." Greta says with an evil smile.

"I'll see if I can get someone to watch the kids." Cheryl says with optimism.

Meanwhile back at the house Danielle is sitting at the dining room table working on her project. She has Ryan's laptop open while she looks up information about the Revolutionary War. Michael is sitting in the great room watching Saturday morning cartoons.

"Danielle, can I have a bowl of Lucky Charms?" Michael asks.

"Sure," Danielle responds.

Michael grabs the cereal out of the cupboard. He pours it into the bowl and adds the milk. He makes a mess while he eats the cereal. After he is done eating, he goes back into the great room. Danielle continues to work on her project with music playing on her headphones. Michael lurks around the great room until he gets an idea. He puts his coat on and sneaks out the front door. Danielle is too busy with her project, the music is so loud that she doesn't hear the door open and close. Michael makes his way to the back shed. He tries to open the door but it's locked. He moves around to the side of the shed and notices a broken window. Michael tries to reach for the window but it's too high. He looks around and sees a large log laying on the ground about ten feet behind the shed. It's around one foot in diameter and two feet long. Michael pushes the log over on its side and rolls it over to the shed. Then he sets the log on one of the flat sides down. He climbs up on the log and looks inside the shed. Michael can see all kinds of old rusted garden tools that haven't been used in years.

"Wow, this is so cool." Michael says as he looks inside the window.

Michael clears the broken glass from the window. Then he climbs through the window sill head first. When he gets inside the window he is dangling down. He is too far in and can't pull himself backwards through the broken window. He tries numerous times to use his legs but they are dangling harmlessly outside the shed. That's until his leg catches a broken piece of glass still in the window frame. The jagged piece of glass rips right through the denim of his blue jeans. The glass begins to dig into his right thighs. Every move he makes the glass digs deeper and deeper.

"Ahh, Danielle help me." Michael yells.

Michael's yells go unheard because he is in the backyard inside the shed and Danielle has her music playing. Michael yells and screams in pain while the piece of glass continues to cut deeper into the muscle. Michael tries to free himself but he doesn't have the leverage. Soon Michael feels wetness on his face. He puts his hands on his face and looks at it.

"Oh my god I'm bleeding. Danielle, Danielle." Michael yells

Michael's yells cannot not be heard by anyone. They are living out by the lake in the country. At this point, Michael begins to panic and with every move he makes the deeper the glass cuts. Soon Michael's blood is dripping into a puddle below his head. Michael is starting to get light headed from being upside down and from the loss of blood. His clothes are soaked in blood and the cold air is making him shiver. Within minutes, Michael starts to go into shock.

In the house, Danielle gets up to go to the bathroom. She walks into the downstairs bathroom and she can hear the TV in the great room. When she finishes up in the bathroom Danielle walks towards the great room.

"It's just a little too quiet in here." Danielle says as she walks into the great room.

She looks around in despair. She walks into the dining room and then the mud room. There is no sign of Michael as she runs up the stairs to the second floor.

"Michael, Michael where the hell are you." Danielle yells out loud.

As panic sets in, Danielle runs through the bedrooms looking in the closets and under the beds. She runs into both upstairs bathroom and still no Michael.

"Michael, this isn't funny, where are you?" Danielle yells as she comes back down the stairs.

Danielle makes it to the bottom stair and sees the front door is unlocked. Without putting on a coat Danielle makes a beeline out the door. She looks out in the front yard and sees nothing. She looks down to the ground at the trace of snow that fell last night. She sees the three sets of foot prints leading into the house and one set off to the side of the house. The shoe prints are small and that tells Danielle they are Michael's prints. Danielle follows Michael's trail as it wanders off into the back yard.

"Michael, where are you?" Danielle yells with her hands cupped together.

Danielle runs following Michael's foot prints. She runs towards the shed and follows the trail around the side of the shed. There she sees a set of legs sticking out the side window. The legs are not moving as Danielle stands on the wooden log.

"Michael, are you alright?" Danielle say as she tries to free him.

Michael is not moving and Danielle tries her hardest to move him. Then she sees the blood dripping down the outside of the shed. Danielle starts to panic and doesn't know what to do. She is not strong enough to lift Michael off the jagged piece of glass. She is scared because Michael is unresponsive and bleeding profusely from his right leg. She goes to the front of the shed and tries to open the locked doors. She pulls with all her might and the two doors handle don't even budge.

"Think Danielle think?" Danielle says to herself.

Quickly she runs into the house and grabs her cell phone that is located on the dining room table. She picks up the phone and dials 911.

"911 dispatch what is your emergency?" The female voice asks.

"My brother he is hanging upside down inside the shed window. He is not moving. Please send help. I can't get inside the shed to help him." Danielle yells as she runs back towards the shed.

"Alright calm down and tell me your name and where you're calling from?" The girl asks.

"My name is Danielle LaRussa. We live at 2430 West Lake Road." Danielle says in panic voice.

"Just calm down Danielle, I have dispatched the fire department. They will be there in about three minutes." The dispatcher says.

Danielle hangs up the cell phone and runs towards Michael again. She picks up a tree branch and starts to swing at the lock on the door. The tree branch breaks with every swing she takes. Hit after hit the brand new lock doesn't budge or break. Danielle is in tears as she tries with all her ability to get into the shed. She doesn't know how long Michael has been out here and she doesn't know the extent of his injuries. Within two minutes she can hear the fire engines sirens off in the distance and nearing quickly. That doesn't stop her from beating on the lock with the branch.

"Michael, can you hear me?" Danielle yells as she keeps beating the lock.

Then the fire truck pulls up in front of the house. Danielle runs out front to meet them as the Lieutenant meets her by the front porch. She explains to him where Michael is as they run around the side of the house towards the back.

"Jimbo, bring the axe." The Lieutenant yells.

One of the firemen grabs the axe off the side of the fire engine. The lieutenant and Danielle arrive first and see Michael's predicament. The lieutenant knows they have to get inside the shed to free him.

"Jimbo, take that door down." The lieutenant yells.

With one swing of the axe the lock goes flying to the ground. Jimbo quickly opens both doors by almost ripping them off the hinges. Jimbo and the lieutenant are the first to enter the shed. They can see Michael is unconscious and unresponsive. There is a small pool of blood that is just over one foot in diameter below Michaels head.

"Jim, give me hand getting him down." The lieutenant says to Jimbo.

Jimbo picks up Michael from around the waist as the lieutenant carefully pulls his leg off the jagged edge of glass. As they are carrying Michael out of the shed, the rescue truck can be heard from a distance. Jimbo sets Michael on the ground while the lieutenant applies pressure to the wound. Another fireman arrives on the scene carrying a large first aid kit. They take out a large roll of gauze and wrap it around Michael's leg. Blood quickly absorbs into the white cotton bandage.

"Is he alive?" Danielle asks emotionally with tears dripping from her eyes.

"He has lost a lot blood but he is alive." The lieutenant says.

Soon the paramedics arrive, followed by the sheriff's department. The paramedics get out of their truck and push the gurney towards the shed. They arrive on the scene as the firemen lift Michael up and on the gurney.

"What do we have here?" One of the paramedics asks the firemen.

"Boy, approximately eight to ten years old." The lieutenant says.

"He is eight." Danielle interrupts.

"A real deep laceration on his right thigh. He has lost a lot of blood." The lieutenant says.

Quickly the paramedics push the gurney towards their truck. They put Michael inside and stabilize him before hooking up an IV. They drive off towards Community Hospital. Danielle grabs her coat and locks up the house. She rides with the sheriff's deputy to the hospital. The fire department picks up and heads back to the station. Danielle explains to the deputy what happened.

"Where are your parents?" The deputy asks Danielle with his lights flashing while heading towards the hospital.

"My mom is working at Boyd's and my father left us last week." Danielle says as she cries out loud.

"Just relax young lady everything will be fine. You did the right thing." The deputy says to Danielle reassuring her.

"I need to call my mom." Danielle says worryingly.

"Don't worry about that I will have a car sent to Boyd's to talk to her." The deputy replies.

The sheriffs calls out to dispatch to send a car to Boyd's and to explain the accident to Cheryl. The sheriffs' car arrives at the hospital and the deputy escorts Danielle to Michael. When she gets there Michael is still unconscious while the doctors is looking at his leg.

"Is he going to be okay?" Danielle asks the doctor.

"He is going to need blood and surgery to repair the muscle in his right thigh." The doctor says.

Within a couple minutes, Cheryl is running down the hall towards Michael's room in the ER. She sees Michael lying on the bed as she falls on her knees at his bed side. She takes hold of his right hand and starts to cry. Danielle sits there with tears in her eyes. She is blaming herself for the accident.

"I'm sorry mom. It's all my fault, I didn't even hear him go outside." Danielle says

"Honey, it's not your fault. If you weren't a caring sister you would have never got up and checked on him." Cheryl replies.

Michael is prepped for surgery. The surgery will repair the shredded muscle in his leg. It's a simple operation but with every surgery there is a risk. Both Cheryl and Danielle sit in the waiting room. The surgery takes about two hours from beginning to end. Cheryl regrets to make this call but she calls Gracie anyways. When she calls it goes right to voice mail. Cheryl leave the message about Michael. After surgery the doctor comes out and tell Cheryl everything went well. He tells her the leg will take about three to four months to heal completely. Cheryl asks the doctor when she can see Michael. He tells her that Michael is in recovery and as soon as he comes around they can sit with him. It has been a long, exhausting, and frustrating day. Cheryl is relieved that the surgery went well as she take a deep breath and a sigh of relief. Then she looks up and Gracie is standing in the doorway to the waiting room.

"Is he going to be alright?" Gracie asks.

"Yes everything went well in surgery." Cheryl replies.

"You should be home with your children. Danielle is too young to watch him." Gracie states with a tone of arrogance.

Cheryl gets up and walks towards Gracie in the doorway. Cheryl has the eyes of a demon as she gets right into Gracie's face.

"Listen hear, I have had enough of your shit. You were too busy with your hair to watch your own grandkids. Your son is a no good piece of shit for abandoning me and the kids. Let alone knocking up some other girl where he used to work. I have to work to support this family. As for Danielle, she is a very good babysitter and she did everything right. If it wasn't for her, Michael would be dead. So why don't you take your selfish ass out of here and leave us alone." Cheryl says in a demanding voice.

Gracie backs down because this is the first time that Cheryl has stood up to her. Gracie undoes her coat and finds a chair in the corner. She sits there for a few minutes to collect her thoughts. About fifteen minutes later a nurse comes down and tells them Michael is in his room and they can visit with him. Cheryl and Danielle get up and follow the nurse. Gracie remains in the chair. She cannot get up for she is embarrassed at her own behavior. When Cheryl and Danielle arrive, Michael is up and aware of his surroundings. He is still a little groggy from the anesthesia. Cheryl and Danielle both give the little man a hug.

"I'm hungry." Michael says.

"What would you like to eat?" Cheryl asks.

"Peanut butter and jelly sandwich with a large glass of milk." Michael replies.

Cheryl is glad that he has his appetite because it's always a good sign. The nurse goes out and gets him his sandwich. Cheryl looks at the bandaged leg that is propped up on a pillow. Within ten minutes, Michael has his sandwich and milk. He eats the sandwich in record time. About an hour later the doctor comes in to check on Michael. He changes the bandage and checks how the wound is healing. He wraps the leg up with a fresh bandage and meets with Cheryl.

"The surgery went well and everything looks good. I want to keep him overnight for observation. You can take him home tomorrow." The doctor says as he shakes Cheryl's hand.

Cheryl tells the doctor thank you. Her and Danielle leave for the night around nine pm. Cheryl reinforces to Danielle that her quick thinking saved Michael's life. They grab a pizza on the way home for dinner and call it an early night.

Chapter 11 – The Homecoming

On Sunday December 7th, Cheryl and Danielle go to mass first thing in the morning. They sit in the back of St. Anthony's parish as Father Angelo gives his sermon. They both listen to the intense reading about giving. Mass lasted about one hour and just like every other mass, Father Angelo leads the procession out of the church. Cheryl and Danielle follow the procession out. They greet Father Angelo at the door.

"It's a shame what happened to Michael. Our almighty father was watching over him that day. How is he doing, my child?" Father Angelo asks Cheryl.

"He is doing good father. He has a very deep laceration on his right leg that needed minor surgery to repair. He is coming home today." Cheryl says with a smile on her face.

"That is good news. I might stop up at the house later if it's okay?" Father Angelo asks.

"That would be nice." Cheryl replies as she heads out the door.

After mass Cheryl drives through at McDonald's. She order a large coffee and Danish for herself. Danielle orders a breakfast sandwich and a small orange juice. They order Michael a sausage with egg biscuit sandwich. Then they head up to the hospital where Michael is still lying in bed. He has a big smile on his face as both Cheryl and Danielle give him a kiss and a hug.

"I hope you bought me something to eat. I'm starving." Michael says as he reaches for the bag.

"Didn't they feed you this morning?" Danielle asks.

"Yeah, but it tasted like crap." Michael replies as he opens the wrapper to the sandwich.

"Where is your breakfast tray?" Cheryl asks.

"They took it away because I ate it all." Michael says as he bites into the sandwich.

The nurse comes in with all the discharge paperwork and instructions. Cheryl signs the paperwork while Michael is helped into a wheelchair. The orderly puts the right foot rest on the wheelchair straight out. He helps Michael out of the bed and into the chair. Michael's right leg is straight out and level. They head down the corridor towards the elevator. The door elevator door opens up and Todd and his new girlfriend are standing together holding hands.

"I see, I'm gone for one week and Michael has a terrible accident and almost dies." Todd says with attitude.

"What are you doing here?" Cheryl asks in an angered tone.

"Visiting my son." Todd replies as he hands Michael a teddy bear.

"How dare you. You and this bimbo take off and leave me absolutely nothing including a place to live. You're a bastard!" Cheryl says as she slaps Todd across the face.

Todd is in shock because he has never seen this side of Cheryl. He stands there motionless, not knowing what to do as the doors on the elevator close. The elevator dings and goes to the next floor.

"We'll take the other elevator." Cheryl says as the adjacent elevator doors open.

The orderly pushes the wheelchair on the other elevator. Cheryl and Danielle follow him on. Just as their doors close on their elevator, Todd's elevator doors open up again. Todd comes running off his elevator just as the doors close in his face. The elevator goes down while Todd has to wait for the next one. When Cheryl reaches the first floor she and the kids make their way to her car. The orderly helps Michael into the front passenger seat. Danielle jumps into the backseat behind the driver's side. The orderly places Michael's injured leg into the car and closes the door behind him. Cheryl walks around to the driver's side when she sees Todd running towards her. Cheryl wants to leave in a hurry because she doesn't want Todd to follow her home. Cheryl is a protective mother and she doesn't want Todd to know where she and the kids are living.

"Wait Cheryl, all I want to do is talk." Todd yells as he runs through the sliding glass doors.

Cheryl starts the car and puts it into drive. Todd reaches out for the door, when all of a sudden he falls to the ground. Todd trips over the same old man that Cheryl has run into at the store. They both fall to the ground and roll over each other on the concrete sidewalk. Cheryl hits the gas pedal as both men tumble to the ground.

"Where did he come from?" Danielle says as she looks out the back window of the car as Cheryl drives away.

"Where did who come from?" Cheryl asks Danielle.

"Dad just collided with some old man. I don't know where the old man came from." Danielle replies.

Cheryl looks out the rearview mirror and sees both Todd and the old man getting up. She drives off quickly so Todd cannot see which direction she is driving.

"You clumsy old man, Why don't you watch where you are going." Todd says to the old man as he gets to his feet.

"I wasn't the one running out of control." The old man replies.

"You filthy old man, why don't you take a bath." Todd says under his breath as he walks away.

Todd walks back inside the hospital to get his pregnant girlfriend. When he gets back outside the old man is nowhere in sight. Todd looks around with a look of surprise on his face.

"What are you looking for?" Prudence asks.

Prudence Jefferies is Todd's pregnant girlfriend. She stands four feet eight inches tall. She is round, plump and caked with makeup. She looks like something from a horror flick. Her hair is tousled and looks a like a bird's nest gone wrong. Her voice is squeaky and she waddles like a duck when she walks. Prudence is a chain smoker and her clothes reek of stale smoke.

"The dirty old man I tripped over." Todd replies.

"Well he isn't here now." Prudence says in her squeaky voice.

Cheryl drives home with a constant eye in her rearview mirror. She makes it home in record time. When she pulls in the driveway she continues to look out her rearview mirror. She won't rest until she gets into house safe and sound. Cheryl gets out of the car and continues looking down the driveway. She helps Michael out of the car where he uses his crutches to get to the house. When they reach the porch steps, Michael sits down and pulls himself up one step at a time. When he gets to the top step Danielle helps him up and hands him his crutches. Cheryl opens the door and continues to look down the driveway.

"What are you looking for?" Danielle asks.

"Your father," Cheryl replies.

"Are you kidding me? You were gone before he even got to his car." Danielle says with a laugh.

They all get into the house where Cheryl locks the door behind her. Danielle helps Michael to one of the couches. Michael sits down and puts his foot up on the ottoman. Danielle turns on the TV. She turns the stations until she finds a football game. The New York Giants are playing against the Dallas Cowboys.

"How about ham and sweet potatoes for dinner?" Cheryl asks.

"Only if we have applesauce." Michael replies.

"I think I can manage that." Cheryl says.

Danielle and Michael sit on the couch and enjoy Sunday football. Danielle plays around with Michael and get him what he needs. She feels responsible for his accident. Cheryl on the other hand prepares a ham dinner. She invites Ryan over for dinner and he accepts. At four thirty Ryan arrives with a bottle chardonnay. He walks into the kitchen as Cheryl is pulling the ham out of the oven.

"Need some help?" Ryan asks.

"Yes please, get the oven door." Cheryl replies.

Ryan rushes over and closes the oven door. Cheryl puts the ham on the counter and places it on a wooden cutting board. Ryan opens the bottle of wine and pours two glasses. Cheryl takes the ham out of the baking dish and sets it on the cutting board.

"Here let me cut that." Ryan says as he takes the knife from Cheryl.

Ryan starts to cut the ham. He does it with expertise as he cuts the meat real thin. Cheryl leans against the counter next to Ryan as he cuts the ham. She has her glass of wine in hand. She sips her wine while they talk about Michael and the court hearing. Ryan cuts off a piece of ham and eats it.

"That's cheating, you're not supposed to eat the ham until we sit down for dinner." Cheryl says as she twists up the kitchen towel.

"I would seriously think about that before you snap it." Ryan says demandingly.

"Really now, is that a threat?" Cheryl says with a smart ass grin.

Before Ryan can answer, she snap the towel across his butt. The towel hits with a loud cracking sound. Ryan puts the knife down and chases Cheryl into the great room. There she stands on the opposite side of the couch of Ryan. Ryan moves to his left and Cheryl would move to her left.

"You might as well give up. I'm going to catch you either way." Ryan says.

"I can't even watch a football game without the older children going at it." Danielle says sarcastically.

After five minutes into the chase Ryan catches Cheryl. He wraps his arms around her and picks her up and carries her into the kitchen. Ryan sets her down and looks into her eyes. He makes his move but Cheryl pulls away.

"I'm not ready for that yet." Cheryl says.

Ryan understands that she has been a through a lot over the past week and a half. He takes it with a grain of salt as he applies a love tap on Cheryl's butt. Cheryl smiles back at Ryan because she hasn't had that type of fun in her life for years.

"Finish cutting that ham or else?" Cheryl says with that evil grin.

"Or else what?" Ryan asks.

"You shall receive another crack across the ass with my magical dish towel." Cheryl says she starts to twirl the towel.

"Promises, promises." Ryan says as he starts to cut the ham again.

On the second slice of meat there a loud crack followed by a stinging sensation. Ryan turns towards Cheryl.

"That hurt." Ryan says while he rubs his butt.

"I know and it sounded good too." Cheryl says with laugh.

They finish up playing around and sit down for dinner. Ryan goes out into the great room and tells the children dinner is ready. Michael hobbles in on his crutches as they sit at the table. Cheryl says grace and everyone digs in. After dinner, they light a fire in the fireplace and put on *Christmas Vacation* with *Chevy Chase*. The whole family including Ryan sits and enjoys the evening together. An evening filled with fun and laughs. By ten pm Ryan makes his way out the door to go home. The kids make their way to bed. Cheryl cleans the kitchen and then makes her way to bed.

Cheryl puts on her pajamas and gets into bed. She turns out the light and reminisces about her and Ryan and how much fun she had with him in the kitchen. She never really had that type of relationship with Todd. Cheryl realizes that she and Ryan have more of an outgoing personality where Todd is more of a manipulator. Cheryl just smiles to herself as she says her prayers and falls asleep before she finishes.

Chapter 12 – The Break In

The next morning, everyone gets up on time for school and work. Cheryl helps Michael down the stairs and into the great room. The doctors want him to stay home on Monday because they want to make sure Michael doesn't move around too much. Too much movement might reopen the wound. Cheryl sets him on the couch with a couple of bottles of water, with a sandwich and chips.

"Make sure the only time you get off the couch is to use the bathroom. Remember to call me at work if something happens. Okay, I love you." Cheryl says to Michael as she kisses him on the forehead.

"Thanks mom, I love you too." Michael replies.

Both Cheryl and Danielle head out the door. Cheryl makes sure she locks the heavy oak door behind her. She drops Danielle off at school before she goes to work.

Cheryl takes her lunch break at noon. She calls home to make sure Michael is okay. Then she goes to the produce department and grabs an apple and an orange. Cheryl pays for the fruit as she sits in a small area for patrons to eat. Greta arrives at work early and she sits at the table with Cheryl. She tells Greta about Michael's accident and his surgery.

"So how are you doing overall?" Greta asks.

"Hanging in there." Cheryl replies.

"So what do think about nerdy Ryan?" Greta says with a smile.

"Nerd no more. He has turned into a hunk." Cheryl says with a grin from ear to ear.

"So you two are hitting it off?" Greta asks with concern.

"No, it's more of a professional relationship. He has been very good to us. He has taken my case, found us a place to live and is he helping out with the kids" Cheryl says.

"He is a good man Cheryl." Greta replies.

Greta heads to the back room to get ready for work. Cheryl eats her orange and places the skin on a napkin on the table. She turns around to throw the orange peels away into a trash can. When she looks forward the old man is standing in front of her table.

"Hi, how are you today?" Cheryl asks.

"I'm good, I'm just returning some cans and bottles. I saw you over here, so I thought I would say hi." The old man replies.

"Do you want a cup of coffee?" Cheryl asks.

"No thank you. How is your son Michael doing?" The old man asks.

Cheryl sits with a puzzling look on her face. She says to herself how does he know about Michaels accident.

"How do you know about that?" Cheryl asks.

"I was here on Saturday when the sheriff's deputy came in to get you. You were in tears." The old man replies.

This put Cheryl's mind at ease as she bites into her apple. The old man walks away towards the back of the store. Cheryl just shrugs it off.

Michael just sits at the house and watches the cartoon network. He eats his sandwich and dozes off a few times. Then at half past one, Michael hears the front door jiggling. Michael sits still and listens. Then he hears it again so he gets up off the couch. He uses his crutches as he hobbles to the front door. He stands there, listens and watches the door handle. Then he sees the door handle moving from side to side. Michael grabs the home phone and heads to the staircase. Michael remains calm and dials 911 while going up the staircase backwards on his butt.

"911, what is your emergency?" The female dispatcher asks.

"Someone is trying to break into the house." Michael says in a panicked voice.

"What's you address?" The dispatcher asks.

"I don't know, we just moved here?" Michael says in despair as he reaches the landing.

Then Michael hears a wood cracking sound. The person outside is using a crow bar to break in. He is wedging the crowbar between the door and frame.

"He is getting in. I can hear the wood breaking on the door." Michael says as he continues to go up the stairs.

"We can trace the call but that is going to take a few minutes." The dispatcher says.

"Wait we called you on Saturday when I got hurt." Michael says as he reaches the top of the stairs.

"2430 West Lake Road. Does that sound right?" The dispatcher asks.

"I don't know but the lake is across the street." Michael says as he goes into his bedroom.

"Find a place to hide, the police are on their way." The dispatcher says as they both hang up.

Michael goes into his room the same time the front door is kicked in. Michael being a smart kid slides into his closet and hides behind the clothes and under some blankets. He can hear the person walking around on the first floor. The intruder's shoes are making noise on the hardwood floor below him. Michael sits still and he can feel his heart thumping in his chest. His mouth is dry and he is scared. Then he hears the person creeping up the stairs. Michael can hear the creaking sound of the wooden stairs. One step at a time the intruder moves up the stairs. Michael stays still and silent. He can hear the intruder when he reaches the top of the stairs. The intruder walks into the master bedroom. Michael is getting nervous because he doesn't hear the police sirens yet. The intruder goes into the master bath and when he comes out he goes into Danielle's bedroom. The person is looking for something because he isn't wrecking the house.

"He is not here." A female voice says.

"Keep looking." A male voice replies.

The voices are muffled to Michael because he is inside the closet and under the blanket. Then one of the intruders enters his bedroom. Michael can hear the footsteps on the hardwood floor. The other one is in the other bathroom as the shower curtain can be heard sliding across the metal bar.

"Look under the bed?" The male voice asks.

"I can't bend down that far." The female responds.

"Get out of my way, you're worthless." The male voice says.

"I hear sirens honey." The female voice says.

"Move it, let's get out of here." The male responds.

The sound of sirens can be heard in the distance. Michael can hear both intruders running down the staircase and across the hardwood floor. They run out the front door and slam it shut. The door is broken so it hits the door frame and flings back into the open position. Michael remains in the closet until he can hear the police enter into the house.

"Hello is there anyone here? This is Deputy Carregher." The police officer yells.

Michael uncovers himself and opens the closet door.

"I'm up here." Michael yells.

Both sheriff's deputies run up the stairs and rescue Michael. They carry him down the stairs and set him on the couch and question him. They ask Michael if he saw the intruders and he tells them no. Michael states that he was hiding in the closet under blankets. Michael tells them he could only hear them walking around and their voices were muffled inside the closet. Michael told the deputies one voice was male and the other female.

"I want my mom." Michael says the deputies.

"She is on her way." Deputy Carregher says.

Just after that Cheryl comes running through the open door. She runs over to Michael and wraps her arms around him.

"Are you alright?" Cheryl asks Michael.

"I'm okay." Michael replies.

"Did you get whoever broke in?" Cheryl asks the deputies.

"No, they were long gone when we got here." Deputy Carregher replies.

"Mom there was a woman and man." Michael interrupts.

Cheryl thinks for a minute while she hold her son. Then it dawn on her.

"It was my ex-husband and his new girlfriend." Cheryl replies.

"How do you know that?" Deputy Carregher asks.

"They want custody of my children." Cheryl replies.

"I think he should have custody of your children. We have been her twice in three days. Both incidents tell me you're not a good parent." Deputy Carregher says out of context.

"What did you say to me?" Cheryl replies in anger.

"Your child almost dies on Saturday. Then you leave him here all alone. Get real ma'am, he is eight years old. I am putting in a complaint to social services that you're an unfit mother." Deputy Carregher states.

"He was fine until someone tried to get in. Secondly have you ever tried to raise children all by yourself? It's not an easy task especially when you're trying to make ends meet on one salary. I am doing my best to raise my children right. Now go find my ex-husband and you will find the people that broke in here." Cheryl yells in a fit of rage.

Both deputies are rendered speechless. They put a call in and start the investigation. Cheryl calls Greta and asks her to pick up Danielle. A locksmith is called to repair the door. Cheryl is upset that Todd can get away with such an act. The house is dusted for prints and a tire mold is made up from the car that the perpetrators were driving. They eliminated the finger prints from Cheryl, Ryan and the kids. They also eliminate police car tire prints along with Ryan's and Cheryl's cars. The locksmith arrives and repairs the door frame. Then he changes out the door lock and adds a dead bolt. Greta drops off Danielle while the investigators are walking through the house and outside on the grounds. Danielle comes into the house and joins Cheryl and Michael on the couch.

"Mom, I heard their voices. The man could have been dad but I can't be sure because everything sounded muffled inside the closet." Michael says.

"I wouldn't put it past him Michael. Tomorrow you can go to school." Cheryl says.

Before the deputies leave for the day, Ryan arrives. He runs in the front door and into the great room.

"Is everyone all right?" Ryan asks.

"We're fine, how did you find out about this?" Cheryl replies.

"Greta called me." Ryan answers.

Cheryl takes Ryan by the arm and they walk into the kitchen.

"This was Todd's doing. I think he was trying to kidnap Michael" Cheryl says to Ryan.

"Why would he do that?" Ryan asks.

"He is afraid he is going to lose the case." Cheryl replies.

"You might have something there. I know he took your saving and he is going to have to give half of that back to you." Ryan says.

"Can you please stay here for the next couple of nights?" Cheryl asks Ryan.

"Yea I can do that. Let me go back to Syracuse to get a few things from my apartment." Ryan replies.

Ryan goes back to his apartment and gets some clothes and his toiletries. When he returns the detectives are just finishing up. The family is all worked up over the ordeal so they decide to go out for dinner. When they return, sleeping arrangement are made. Ryan will sleep on the couch just in case anyone else decides to break in during the night. By ten pm both kids are in bed sleeping while Cheryl and Ryan talk.

"Why is Todd doing this to us?" Cheryl asks Ryan.

"He is desperate. He is trying to get to you." Ryan replies.

"I don't understand. When we were marred I did whatever I could for him." Cheryl says as she starts to cry.

"Come on Cheryl, just relax. Nothing else is going to happen. I'm here and if anyone comes in that door, they're going to get this Louisville Slugger upside their head." Ryan says with the wooden baseball bat at his side.

"You're going hit a homerun!" Cheryl says with a smile as she lays her head onto Ryan's shoulder.

"No, not just a homerun but a grand slam. You need to calm down everything will be fine. Mark my words on that." Ryan replies as he holds her tight.

Ryan and Cheryl sit together on the couch. Cheryl grabs the remote and turns on the TV. She flips from station to station until reaches TCM.

"Wow, this is the old version of a Christmas Carol." Cheryl says.

"I remember seeing this version with my dad." Ryan says with a smile.

"What year was this made?" Cheryl asks before she pushes the info button.

"1938 and Reginald Owen portrays Ebenezer Scrooge." Ryan says with a smile.

"Do you want to watch it?" Cheryl asks.

"I sure do." Ryan replies.

"Then let's do it right." Cheryl says.

Ryan looks at Cheryl not sure what she means. Cheryl gets up off the couch and turns off the lights and plugs in the Christmas tree. She grabs an afghan and puts it around her and Ryan.

"This is the way this movie needs to be watched. All cuddled up under an afghan with only the Christmas tree lights glowing." Cheryl says as she lays her head on Ryan's shoulder.

Chapter 13 – Tuesday December 9th

The next morning, Cheryl and Ryan are still on the couch all cuddled up under the afghan. Cheryl wakes up with sleep still in her eyes. She looks over at Ryan and she can see he is staring at her. Cheryl rubs her eyes and smiles at Ryan.

"Why are you staring at me?" Cheryl asks.

"You're just as beautiful sleeping as you are when you're awake." Ryan says with a smile.

"That's so sweet." Cheryl replies with a peck on Ryan's cheek.

"You know I had a crush on you all through school. I bet you didn't know that?" Ryan's says.

"How was I supposed to know that you liked me? You never even said a word to me when we were in school." Cheryl says.

"I was shy, and I was afraid you would say no if I asked you out." Ryan replies.

"You're probably right, you were nerdy with glasses and that wasn't my type." Cheryl says with a laugh.

"Why you," Ryan says as he starts to tickle Cheryl behind her knees.

Cheryl squirms around and laughs while Ryan tickles her. She tries to get away but Ryan hold her down.

"Please, please I have, have to get the kids ready for school." Cheryl says as she stutters while laughing.

"What's the matter you can dish it out but you can't take it." Ryan says as he continues to tickle her.

Finally, Ryan lets Cheryl go. She gets out from underneath the afghan and walks towards the stairs. She starts to jog up the stairs.

"Let's go children time to get up. Let's go, you have school today." Cheryl yells as she gets to the landing at the top of the stairs.

Ryan gets up and folds up the afghan. He goes into the kitchen and takes out the pancake mix. He hears the shower turn on and the sound of footsteps walking around above him on the second floor. Ryan smiles as he puts all the ingredients into the mixing bowl. Then he can hear *Taylor Swift* music coming from upstairs. Ryan pulls out a whisk and starts to beat up the batter. He throws a large skillet on the stovetop and turns on the heat. He throws margarine in the skillet and watches it melt. Ryan pours the first cup of the batter into the skillet. He watches as the batter starts to bubble. Then he flips the pancake over in the skillet by just flipping his wrists. The pancake makes a perfect landing back into the skillet.

"What smells so good?" Michael asks as he walks in the kitchen on his crutches.

"That would be my world famous chocolate chip pancakes. They are only served in my kitchen." Ryan says as he puts the first pancake on a plate.

"Can I have one?" Michael asks as he sits down on a stool located on the island in the kitchen.

"Here you go sir. Would you like some maple syrup to go with your pancake?" Ryan says in a disguised waiter's voice.

"You're funny Ryan." Michael says while laughing.

A few minutes later Danielle and Cheryl arrive in the kitchen. Danielle grabs a plate and takes two pancakes for herself. Cheryl only takes one while Ryan finishes cooking the final pancake. Ryan grabs a plate and takes the final two pancakes. He takes a seat next to the girls at the dining room table.

"These are good. Where did you learn how to make these?" Cheryl asks.

"Ahh ancient Ryan secret." Ryan responds.

"You know you're so full of it." Danielle says.

"No Danielle, he is full of himself." Cheryl replies.

Both Cheryl and Danielle laugh out loud. Michael looks on like someone died. Michael doesn't know what was so funny about that joke. Ryan sits at the table with a smirk on his face that goes from ear to ear. After breakfast Ryan cleans up while Cheryl takes the children to school. He cleans up in the bathroom before he heads to work in Syracuse.

The day goes by with less drama then previous days. At the end of the day Cheryl leaves work to get the kids from school. She has a good day with less complaining customers. She puts on her coat as she walks out the front door. The temperature is about forty degrees with dark gray clouds in the sky.

"Looks like it's going to rain." The old man says as he startles Cheryl.

"Whoa, you scared me. I think you're right, rain is in the forecast." Cheryl replies.

"Miss, could you please give me ride?" The old man asks.

"Sure, where would you like to go?" Cheryl asks.

"Can you take me to the hospital?" The old man asks.

"Is everything alright. Are you okay?" Cheryl asks with anticipation.

"Oh, I'm fine. There is someone there I want to see." The old man replies.

Cheryl unlocks the car doors as they both get in. Cheryl starts the car and puts it into drive. She drives out of the parking lot and onto the main road.

"So, who do you need to see?" Cheryl asks.

"Someone that has been asking for guidance." The old man replies.

"What are you a priest or something?" Cheryl asks as she turns onto the road where the hospital is located.

"A priest oh no, no, no. Something, yes I would have to agree to that." The old man says with laughter.

Cheryl has a look of surprise on her face because she doesn't know how to take that answer. She quickly turns the car into the front area of the hospital. She unlocks the car doors.

"Here you go. I hope your friend is okay." Cheryl says as the old man opens the car door.

"He will be fine. Thank you very much for the ride. I will tell you one thing Cheryl LaRussa, you a very good person with a big heart. Mark my words, things are not as bad as you think." The old man says as he shuts the car door.

Before Cheryl can answer the old man, he starts to walk away. Cheryl turns off the car and gets out. She comes around the front of her car as she drops her keys. Cheryl bends down and picks up her keys. She runs towards the hospital door. She opens the front door to the hospital looking for the old man. She runs inside and looks down the corridor and only sees hospital staff and patients. Cheryl turns her head from side to side and the old man is nowhere to be seen. Cheryl walks up to the information desk.

"Did you just see a little old man come in here?" Cheryl asks.

"Miss, a lot of people come through that door. Most of the time I'm not paying attention." The young girl replies.

Cheryl looks around a little bit more. Then she turns around and heads towards the door.

"That old man moves awful quickly!" Cheryl states to the girl behind the desk.

The girl behind the desk shakes her head. She must be thinking Cheryl is off her rocker.

Cheryl turns and walks out the door. She gets into her car and goes to pick up the kids from school. She goes to pick Danielle up first and waits out front of the junior high school. Danielle comes out of the school and runs over to the car and gets in. Then Cheryl heads to the elementary school where they both have to help Michael into the car. When everyone is in the car and ready to go Michael asks a question.

"Mom, can we have pizza for dinner?" Michael asks.

"Sure, why not." Cheryl replies as she pulls out her cell phone.

Cheryl calls and places an order for an extra-large cheese pizza and a small mushroom pizza. On their way home they pick up the pizza with a two liter bottle of Pepsi. They make their way home and sit at the dining room table eating the pizza and drinking the Pepsi.

"Mom do you think Santa will bring me the Xbox One that I want for Christmas?" Michael asks.

"I don't know honey." Cheryl replies.

"You keep asking for it, I think Santa will hear you." Danielle says to keep Michaels hopes up.

Cheryl looks over at Danielle with burning eyes. Cheryl knows she cannot afford a four hundred dollar game system. She is barely able to keep food on the table. As the conversation comes to an end, someone knocks on the front door. Cheryl looks out the dining room window and see a silhouette of a woman standing on the porch.

"Who is it mom?" Danielle asks.

"I don't know who it is, it's too dark outside to make out." Cheryl replies as she puts the curtain back in place.

Cheryl walks over to the door and turns on the outside porch light. She looks through the glass and see Grandma Gracie standing there with a cigarette dangling out of her mouth. Cheryl is hesitant at first but she opens the door.

"No smoking in here Gracie. It's not my house." Cheryl says to Gracie.

"That figures. It's getting ridiculous, you can't smoke anywhere." Gracie replies as she throws her cigarette into the lawn.

"What do you want?" Cheryl asks as Gracie walks in.

"I don't know what my son ever saw in you. I wouldn't mind but you're not even that pretty." Gracie says as she passes by Cheryl.

Cheryl is left speechless from the embarrassing statement that just came out of Gracie's mouth. Cheryl would like to belt Gracie, but she holds her composure. Gracie walks into the dining room to see the kids. She gives them a hug and kiss while sitting down.

"Would you like a slice of pizza?" Cheryl asks.

"I don't mind if I do." Gracie replies.

Cheryl sets a plate in front of Gracie. She grabs a piece of mushroom pizza. She takes a bite and shakes her head stating she likes it. Cheryl pours Gracie a glass of Pepsi.

"Nice place you have here?" Gracie says as she looks around.

"Gracie, this is only temporary. The people that own the house live in Florida during the winter. Now, what is the reason for your visit?" Cheryl says.

"Well, Todd would like to see the kids." Gracie asks.

"He is going to have to wait until the weekend. They have homework to do and tomorrow is a school day." Cheryl replies.

"Well, Todd is out in the car and he wants to see them?" Gracie demands.

"You go tell Todd to stick it up his ass. I have my assumptions that he and his new girlfriend were the two people that broke into this house. Tell him that the sheriff's department is investigating the break in and he is the number one suspect. Now take your pizza and get out of the house." Cheryl says as she raises her voice.

Gracie gets up and doesn't say a word. She zips her coat up and walks out the front door with her eyes and head looking straight forward.

"What a prude you are." Cheryl says as she slams the door behind Gracie.

Cheryl locks the door just as it latches. Cheryl is aware of what is going to happen next. Sure enough she hears the car door slam. Someone walks up the wooden steps slamming their feet down hard on the wooden porch deck. Then there is a loud banging on the door.

"Cheryl, open the door. I have a right to see my own children." Todd yells.

"You lost that right two week ago when you walked out on them." Cheryl yells back at Todd.

"You either open this door or I will smash it in." Todd yells as his anger grows.

"What are you going to do, smash it in like you did a couple of days ago?" Cheryl replies.

"That's it." Todd yells as he kicks the door in.

Cheryl jumps backwards as the door flings open. The glass shatters inwards towards Cheryl as she puts her arms up to protect her face from the flying shards. The flying glass hits her arms and a few pieces hit her face before the glass falls to the floor. The kids are in the dining room and they start to yell.

"Call 911," Cheryl yells to Danielle.

Todd grabs Cheryl around the neck and lifts her off the floor. His grasp is so tight that he squeezes her throat with all his strength. Cheryl tries to gasp for air but her airway is restricted. Both kids are in a panicked state as they yell and scream in terror. Michael yells and screams at his father to let her go, but he disregards the pleas from the distressed child.

"What's the matter honey? Having a hard time breathing." Todd says as he puts his face into hers.

Todd pushes Cheryl against the wall and continues to strangle her. Cheryl fights and kicks to get away from Todd. Todd squeezes Cheryl's neck like a crazed man. Todd doesn't let go as he crushes her air passage. Danielle finishes making the call to 911 but by the time they arrive Cheryl will be dead.

"Dad let her go." Danielle yells.

Todd doesn't pay attention to his screaming kids as he takes his frustration out on Cheryl. Cheryl's face is turning red from the lack of oxygen. Then car headlights can be seen pulling into the driveway. A car door shuts and Cheryl hears the sound of someone sprinting up the porch stairs. Todd ignores the sound coming up from behind him. Before anything can be said Todd feels a belt of pain across the back of his head. He drops Cheryl to the ground and he turns towards the door. Todd doesn't even see the second hit that crushes his nose. Todd flies backwards and over the top of Cheryl as his head hits the hardwood floor. Todd's head bounces off the floor and before he can see what hit him, Ryan is on top of him. Ryan lets loose, belt after belt into Todd's face. After the third hit Todd is out for the count. Cheryl leans against the wall and grabs her neck while she tries to catch her breath. Ryan gets off Todd and he runs over to Cheryl aid.

"Come on honey, breath." Ryan says as he pulls Cheryl up into a sitting position.

"Mom, are you alright?" Danielle asks as she run over to her mother's side.

Within a couple of minutes Cheryl is breathing normal. Ryan helps her to the couch when the sheriff's deputies arrives. The two armed men enter the house with their guns drawn. They see Todd lying on the floor unconscious with a bloodied face.

"Hold it right there!" The deputy yells at Ryan.

"The man you want is on the floor. I want him charged with breaking and entering, aggravated assault, along with attempted murder." Ryan says as he applies an ice pack on Cheryl throat.

"What are you a lawyer or police officer?" The deputy asks.

"I'm a lawyer and if I didn't show up when I did, this young lady would be dead." Ryan states.

Both deputies handcuff Todd and take him away. Cheryl's neck is sore and she is frightened from the ordeal. She never imagined Todd would go that far. Outside Gracie can be heard yelling at the deputies as they put Todd in the squad car. When the sheriff's car leaves Gracie follows close behind them.

"Thank you," Cheryl says to Ryan.

"I can't stand to see what this man is putting you through. If you don't mind I would like to sleep on your couch until this ordeal is over with." Ryan says.

Cheryl agrees with Ryan because Todd has become unpredictable. The safety of the children is her number one fear. If Todd could do this to her, what can he do to the kids. A couple minutes later another deputy arrives and takes Cheryl's statement.

When the deputy leaves Ryan tries to close and lock the front door. The door frame is destroyed and the door will not latch or lock. Ryan rigs the door closed with wood planks nailed into the wall and door frame. After all the commotion, they finish up dinner and watch a little TV. The kids go to bed around nine thirty pm and Cheryl decides to takes a bath. After a long and soothing bath she takes a couple of aspirin and goes right to bed. Ryan cleans up the dinner dishes and loads up the dishwasher. Then Ryan packs it in for the night on one of the couches in the great room. He wraps himself up in a blanket and gets comfortable and within a few minutes he passes out.

Chapter 14 – Charges Brought Up?

The next morning Ryan is out of bed at the crack of dawn. He races down to county sheriff's department to press charges on Todd. When he arrives at the sheriff's department to his surprise, there is no record of Todd being arrested. It was like nothing ever happened. Ryan wants to go right to the sheriff himself to find out why Todd was set free. Ryan asks the desk sergeant to see the arrest report and he is given the run around.

"Let me talk to Sheriff Jones?" Ryan demands to the desk sergeant.

"He is busy right now." The desk sergeant replies.

"I demand to see him right now." Ryan says as he gets into the desk sergeants face.

"I told you he was busy and if you don't back down I will have you arrested." The desk sergeant says as he stands up.

"Okay, just answer me one question. What charges were brought up against Todd LaRussa? Your deputies handcuffed him on West Lake Road last night. He was choking his wife to death when I arrived and broke it up." Ryan says a calm voice.

The desk sergeant goes through the paperwork on his desk. He finds the arrest report and takes a look at it. He gives it to Ryan and he reads the report quickly. His eye movements and facial expressions show his dissatisfaction as he is reads the document. The desk sergeant can see in Ryan's eyes that he is starting to get upset.

"Todd LaRussa was arrested last night for breaking and entering only. A misdemeanor charge that he made bail on last night. There is nothing here about attempted murder." Ryan says as the Sheriff opens his office door.

"Attempted murder." Sheriff Jones says.

Sheriff Jones is a six feet three inch tall black man. He had broad shoulders and a round belly. The sixty one year old man has salt and pepper hair that is cut very short to his head. He sports a mustache that is also salt in pepper in color. He dresses in his khaki colored uniform accompanied by black boots.

"Yes, last night Cheryl LaRussa was attacked by her ex-husband. He had her in a strangle hold when I arrived." Ryan says.

"And who are you?" Sheriff Jones asks.

"Ryan DeCicero, and I am Cheryl's lawyer." Ryan replies.

Sheriff Jones takes the arrest report from Ryan. He asks Ryan to come into his office. He looks at the arrest report with angry eyes. He reads through the report thoroughly.

"My deputies do not mention a thing about attempted murder in this report. All they have in here is breaking and entering with minimal damage." The sheriff says as he looks up at Ryan.

"Minimal damage. The man broke down the door. He sought out his ex-wife inside the house. When he found her, he grabbed her around the neck and lifted her off the floor. He had such a tight grip around her neck, Cheryl has dark and deep bruises that are revealing. You call that minimal damage. I want this man arrested for unlawful entry, breaking and entering, aggravated assault and attempted murder." Ryan states.

"I am personally going to look into this." Sheriff Jones says as he escorts Ryan to the door.

"Thank you," Ryan says as he heads out the door.

"I want both Mendez and Reynolds in my office before they start their shift." Sheriff Jones says to the desk sergeant.

Ryan bundles up as he heads out of the sheriff's department. It's a cold and blustery day with gray skies. Ryan calls Cheryl on her cell phone to let her know about the sheriff's department blunders. Cheryl has taken the kids to school and then she goes back home to rest. She is taking the day off from work as she tries to recuperate from last night's attack. Ryan goes to Lowes and buys a new front door. He has it delivered the same day after he explains to the manager what happened. Ryan heads back to Cheryl's house where he calls out sick to his assistant. When he pulls into the driveway he parks right behind Cheryl's car. Ryan walks in the house through the back door where he sees Cheryl cooking up a few eggs.

"Are you hungry? Would you like a couple of scrambled eggs?" Cheryl asks.

"Sounds good to me." Ryan replies.

"Are you going to work today?" Cheryl asks as flips the eggs over.

"No I called in today. I want to be here for you and I also have a new door being delivered and installed." Ryan replies.

"Ryan, I can't afford that right now." Cheryl replies.

"Don't worry about it. You can pay me back when you get the cash." Ryan says as he takes his coat off and takes a seat at the island.

Cheryl finishes cooking the eggs and sets them onto two plates. The toaster pops and she butters all four pieces. She gives Ryan two slices of toast and keeps two for herself.

"Would you like a cup of coffee?" Cheryl asks.

"I sure would. Hopefully it's strong enough to wake me up." Ryan responds as he starts to eat the eggs.

Cheryl sits next to Ryan. She picks at her food while Ryan gobbles down the eggs and toast in record time. Cheryl sits with both hands on her mug while she gazes over at Ryan. She absorbs the aura of the moment because she and Todd never had a relaxing breakfast together. Todd always ate his food and ran out the door on his merry way.

"Wow, these eggs are good." Todd says as he takes a sip of coffee.

"I'm glad you like them. How's the coffee?" Cheryl asks.

"Whoa, that is strong!" Ryan says after one sip of the coffee.

The morning goes by and the Lowes truck arrives. They tear off the old door and frame in record time. Then they put up the new frame and install the door. Cheryl feels the house cooling down from the open door, so she decides to light a fire in the fireplace. This will help stave off the cold from infiltrating throughout the house. Ryan works along with the installers because he likes to do handyman work. Cheryl sits on the couch with both hands covering her coffee mug. She sits with an afghan around her shoulders. She looks on and admires the way Ryan works. Cheryl smiles at Ryan when he turns back to look at her. Ryan always gives her a funny face and she laughs at him. The installation takes about two hours. When the job is complete the door is reinforced with two deadbolt locks, a chain lock and a door wedge. The door wedge is a metal bar that hooks into a metal bracket located just below the door handle. The wedge hooks into a metal bracket located in the wooden floor. The installation guys are so thorough they even take all the scrap from the old door.

"I would like to see Todd put his shoulder into this door. He is going to dislocate his shoulder or break a bone trying." Ryan says with laughter.

Ryan turns both dead bolt locks and wedges the metal bar in place.

"It's going to take an act of God to break down this door." Ryan says to Cheryl.

"Well at least I will sleep a little better tonight. That doesn't mean that Todd won't break a window to get in." Cheryl replies to Ryan.

"If he does, I will be there." Ryan replies

Cheryl decides to take a shower. Ryan grabs the rest of the coffee and takes a seat on the couch. Just as he starts to relax his cell phone rings. He looks at the screen and sees it's the sheriff's department calling.

"Hello," Ryan says.

"Hi Mr. DeCicero, this is Sheriff Jones." Sheriff Jones says.

"Hi sheriff, what can I do for you?" Ryan asks.

"I'm looking into your complaint from this morning. I called and talked to the two arresting deputies and they are both holding to their story. They both are saying Todd was arrested for breaking and entering." The sheriff says.

"What? They are lying sheriff." Ryan says in a fit of rage.

"Hold your horses there Ryan and let me finish. I did a little investigation on both of these deputies and I'm finding a link between them and Todd LaRussa. It seems that Todd and both my deputies are working together in a skimming operation with Todd's old dealership. They have been stealing thousands of dollars." Sheriff Jones states.

"Then why in hell haven't they been arrested?" Ryan asks with concern.

"There is an ongoing investigation that the FBI is conducting. I am just getting wind of it now because the FBI is waiting to get all the facts and everyone involved. As soon as my deputies arrive for their shift they are going to be arrested. I put out an APB on Todd LaRussa and as soon as he is found he is going to be arrested too for grand larceny." Sheriff Jones says with confidence.

"What about the four charges from yesterday?" Ryan asks.

"Who are you taking too Ryan?" Cheryl asks as she comes down the stairs fully dressed and her hair wrapped in a towel.

Ryan puts his finger up his mouth instructing Cheryl to keep her voice down.

"Those charges are going to be added to Todd as soon as we apprehend him." Sheriff Jones says.

"I will be following up on that." Ryan states.

"I expect no less. One more thing, I would like someone to stay with Mrs. LaRussa. I think Todd is reckless and dangerous. If he gets wind of this he is going to make one last ditch effort to try and kill her and take the kids." Sheriff Jones says.

"Sheriff, I am going to be staying here. How about if you posting a car here with a few deputies?" Ryan says.

"I can do that. I think we will apprehend Todd very quickly." Sheriff Jones replies.

The sheriff and Ryan agree the deputies will be placed at the house immediately.

"Who was that?" Cheryl asks.

"That was sheriff and your ex is in deeper trouble than we thought." Ryan says.

Ryan explains to Cheryl what is going on. She knew Todd was up to no good but couldn't put a finger on it. Ryan told her that the sheriff wants to post a car outside. Ryan reassures Cheryl that Todd will not get into the house. Cheryl agrees with Ryan and supports the extra safety measures. Ryan and Cheryl drive to Syracuse to get more of Ryan's belongings from his apartment. While driving home Ryan calls his office and tells his assistant that he will be taking a leave of absence. He instructs her to transfer all his cases to his partner. When they return from Syracuse they pick up the kids from school and go out to dinner. After dinner they return home, where the house is locked down like a fort. Both Danielle and Michael are instructed not to go near their father. They both agree with their mom and Ryan that their father has issues. Both Danielle and Michael witnessed what their father is capable of. His actions from the night before are inexcusable and warrant safety precautions.

Chapter 15 – Thursday December 11th

Ryan is awakened the next morning at four o'clock with his cell phone ringing. He looks at the screen and sees the sheriff department calling in.

"Hello," Ryan says in a sleepy voice.

"Ryan, its Sheriff Jones. I'm sorry to call you at such and early hour. I have new information on your case. First of all, both my deputies have been arrested by the FBI. They are chirping like jail birds to save themselves some prison time. Secondly, I honored my promise and I have a car parked in your driveway." Sheriff Jones says.

"Very good the more protection here the better I feel" Ryan says as he gets up from the couch and looks out the front window.

Ryan can see the sheriff's car parked in the driveway with two silhouettes sitting in the front seat. Ryan moves back towards the couch and he hears someone moving upstairs. It's coming from the master bedroom which tells him that Cheryl is stirring.

"Well the main reason I'm calling you as we had a run with Todd tonight. We were going to apprehend him outside his mother's house and shots were fired. He wounded one of my deputies but Todd got away. He is now considered armed and dangerous. I will keep my deputies at the house until we apprehend Todd." Sheriff Jones says.

"Thanks for the information." Ryan says.

"Keep an eye open for him. Stay safe and I will be in touch." Sheriff Jones says as he hangs up.

"Who was that?" Cheryl says from the stairway.

"Your ex has a gun and he shot and wounded a deputy. They didn't apprehend him so Todd is on the loose. The sheriff has a car parked in the driveway for our safety. We need to keep an eye on the kids. No telling what Todd is capable of now because he is a fugitive on the run." Ryan says.

"What are we going to do?" Cheryl says panicking.

"Cheryl, he is on the run. If he stays in this area he will be caught sooner than later. He has the city police, the sheriff's department, the state police and the FBI looking for him." Ryan says with confidence.

Cheryl goes upstairs to bed but she is unable to fall back asleep. The next morning she and Ryan take the kids to school with the sheriff's car following close behind them. After that Cheryl makes an unscheduled stop at St Anthony's church. She goes inside the church and puts her hand in the holy water and does the sign of the cross. She makes her way up to the front of the church and bows to the altar before she steps into one of the pews. Again she does the sign of the cross as she goes down onto her knees to pray. Cheryl says five or six prayers before she starts to talk to Jesus.

"Dear Lord, I know I have been a good woman. I try to raise my children the catholic way. I teach them right from wrong and good from bad. I am here today to ask you to please protect them from Todd. If you need to take someone please take me and spare my children. I am so afraid of what he is capable of. Please I ask with all my heart to protect them from the evil that Todd has become." Cheryl says before she says another five or six prayers.

Cheryl gets up and kneels down and does the sign of the cross and she exits the pew. She walks towards the back of the church where Ryan is standing. She looks up into the balcony and the old man standing there. He smiles down at her as he puts his hand up to wave. Cheryl waves back to him. Ryan see this and he emerges from underneath the baloney to look up at a vacant balcony. He looks back at Cheryl with a look of surprise. They exit the church and get into the car.

"Who did you wave at in the balcony?" Ryan asks.

"The old man." Cheryl replies.

Ryan doesn't say a word and hopes she isn't losing it. He drives Cheryl to work and before she gets out of the car she kisses Ryan on the cheek.

"Thank you for being here for us." Cheryl says.

"It's my pleasure." Ryan replies.

Ryan goes back to house where he works on Cheryl's divorce and custody case. These new charges against Todd will definitely revoke any rights for him. Ryan wants to make sure he has water tight case for Cheryl. Ryan sees the love in Cheryl's eyes for her children. He is going to make sure she gets everything she deserves. Ryan works all day on the case until he realizes how fast time has flown by. He runs out to his car and drives to the middle school. He picks up Danielle with the sheriff car on his tail. He has about forty minutes until Michael gets out.

"Hey what do you think your mother wants for Christmas?" Ryan asks Danielle.

"I don't know? Have you asked her?" Danielle replies.

"Well, I want to buy her something nice." Ryan says with smile.

"You know my father hasn't bought her anything nice in years. He would always buy her a commodity item that he could use too. You could buy her a small piece of jewelry. The only jewelry she has is her engagement and wedding ring." Danielle replies.

"Jewelry it is. Come on we have about thirty minutes before Michael get out." Ryan says as he put the car in gear.

Ryan drives down to the mall and goes into the jewelry store. He looks at all kinds of ear rings and necklaces. Then he see a beautiful heart shaped pendant on a solid gold chain. The heart is covered with rubies that surrounds a diamond. Ryan falls in love with this piece of jewelry as he holds it in his hand.

"What do you think of this?" Ryan asks Danielle.

"It's absolutely beautiful, mom will love it." Danielle replies,

Ryan buys the necklace and has the girls wrap it up. The girl asks him if wants insurance on the jewelry and Ryan declines.

"You know mom is falling in love with you." Danielle says.

"Where did that come from?" Ryan asks in shock.

"Are you that blind? I can see it her eyes when she looks at you." Danielle says with a smile.

"Okay, let's not get ahead of ourselves here." Ryan says as he tries to change the subject.

"It's true Ryan. You treat Michael and me like we are your own children. Mom has never had anyone pay as much attention to her like you do." Danielle replies.

"How old are you?" Ryan asks.

"Thirteen why?" Danielle responds.

"Are sure you're not thirty." Ryan says with laughter.

"My mom says I'm thirteen going on thirty-five." Danielle says with a smile.

After the gift is wrapped, they go and pick up Michael at the elementary school. Danielle and Ryan have to help him to the car. The sheriff's car is still following close behind them. The next stop is Boyd's to pick up Cheryl. When they arrive they have to wait a few minutes in the parking lot.

"How would you two like to do something fun this evening?" Ryan asks.

"What did you have in mind?" Danielle asks.

"Roller skating or something like that?" Ryan replies.

"Really, is that supposed to be funny?" Michael says with his crutches in hand.

"Well Michael what would you like to do?" Ryan asks.

"How about some fast food and then we catch a movie." Michael replies.

"I'm in for that. How about you Danielle?" Ryan says.

"I liked the roller skating idea or better yet ice skating. But I guess a movie would be good thanks to gimpy." Danielle says jokingly.

"Okay we do this for Michael tonight and guess what Danielle, you and I will go ice skating on Saturday." Ryan replies.

"Yes, sounds like a plan to me." Danielle says as Cheryl gets into the car.

"What sounds like a plan?" Cheryl asks.

"Tonight were going out for fast food and then we are catching a movie. On Saturday I'm taking Danielle ice skating. Would you like to join us?" Ryan says with a smile.

"Oh my god, I haven't been ice skating since I was eighteen years old." Cheryl replies.

"You didn't answer the question, do you want to go or not?" Ryan asks.

"I would love to go." Cheryl replies.

They hit up Burger King for dinner. Then it's off to the movies to see the new release of *The Avengers II*. Ryan pays for everything as they go into the theatre. Cheryl and the kids walk towards the theatre as Ryan goes over to the concession stand.

"What are you doing?" Cheryl asks.

"Can't watch a movie without popcorn and coke." Ryan says as he order four drinks and an extra-large popcorn.

When the movies is over they head home with the sheriffs car still following them. They get into the house where everyone grabs a snack before bed. They all huddle in the great room and watch the movie *Scrooged* with *Bill Murray*. They are in stiches because this is the first time that Danielle and Michael have ever seen the comedy.

"Would you like a glass of wine?" Cheryl asks Ryan.

"Not really but I would love a beer." Ryan replies.

"I think I can handle that." Cheryl says.

Cheryl lets the kids stay up until eleven o'clock to watch the end of the movie. When the movie ends she walks them up the stairs and helps Michael into his pajamas. She tucks Michael in and kisses him on the forehead. Cheryl goes over to Danielle room and peeks inside. Danielle is already in bed and turning out the lamp on the night stand.

"You know mom, I like Ryan. He likes to do things with us." Danielle says with a grin from ear to ear.

"I kind of like him too." Cheryl says.

"I can see that twinkle in your eyes mom. I think he is a keeper. He treats you like gold." Danielle says as she turns out the light.

"Yeah honey, I think you may be right. Good night." Cheryl says as she closes the bedroom door.

"Good night mom." Danielle says as the door latches.

Cheryl and Ryan sit on the couch watching reruns of *The Big Bang Theory*. They cuddle up and laugh in harmony. Then Ryan turns his head towards Cheryl who is gazing at him. He doesn't say a word as their lips meet. He kisses her deeply and passionately for the first time. Cheryl kisses back and for the first time in her life she feels the kiss of love. When they finally break away Cheryl puts her arms around Ryan and hugs him as tight as she can.

"That was nice." Cheryl says as she nibbles at Ryan's ear.

They hold each other tight and cuddle for a few minutes. Cheryl rests her head on Ryan's shoulder as she caresses his back.

"I hope there are more kisses like that?" Ryan asks as he kisses her gently on the lips.

"There will be, remember I'm still a married woman." Cheryl says in humorous manner.

"As of next Tuesday you won't be." Ryan replies.

"I guess I'm going to have to remember that." Cheryl says with a smile.

Cheryl gets up off the couch and kisses Ryan one last time for the night.

"Good night, my knight in shining armor." Cheryl says as she heads for the stairs.

"Good night my queen." Ryan replies as Cheryl smiles back and starts to climb up the stairs.

Ryan gets up and puts the beer bottle and wine glass into the sink. He walks around the downstairs to make sure everything is locked up. He even put the metal wedge in place to prevent a break in. Ryan takes one last look outside and he sees the sheriff's car running with the head lights off. He shuts off the lights, TV and cuddles under the afghan. Ryan is totally exhausted from the early morning call. He closes his eyes and wishes this family could be his.

"Good night my queen. I could have said something better than that. I should have said good night my beautiful and wife to be." Ryan whispers to himself in the dark.

Little did Ryan know Cheryl was sitting at the top of the stairs listening to him? Cheryl smiles and makes her way to her bedroom. She turns off the lights with the biggest smile on her face. She stretches her legs and arms before she cuddles under her sheets and comforter. She says her prayers and fall asleep.

Chapter 16 – Gracie's Betrayal

On Friday morning, things go as usual. Cheryl goes to work and the kids go to school. The kids are only one week away from Christmas vacation. Ryan remains at the house on the lake preparing his custody case for Cheryl. Todd is at large with his girlfriend Prudence. Gracie on the other hand, has been to the sheriff's department a couple of times. They keep asking her questions on Todd's whereabouts. She sticks with her son and continues to give the same answers. The sheriff's department keeps a close eye on Gracie and her home, just in case Todd stops by.

Cheryl on the other hand, is busy with the craziness that comes with the Christmas season working at a store. She likes to work because it takes her mind off everything going on. Cheryl worries about buying Christmas presents for the kids because they require a lot of money to buy them. Cheryl's biggest worry is thinking about a permanent place to live. Cheryl knows money is tight with just one income and two children. This is a mother's worst nightmare unfolding right in front of her very own eyes. When lunch time comes, Cheryl eats right at Boyd's. She sits at the table eating a large salad and a piece of Italian bread. Greta starts walking by and sees Cheryl. Greta stops at her table and starts a conversation.

"Do you mind if I join you?" Greta asks.

"Sure, pull up a chair." Cheryl responds.

"How's Michael doing?" Greta asks.

"The injury is healing but he is still having a hard time walking. I think another week or so before he is up and around again." Cheryl replies with a smile.

"Boy, those bruises on your neck look painful." Greta says with a sour look on her face.

"It's not that bad now. They really hurt yesterday." Cheryl says as she closes the scarf on her neck to hide the bruises.

"Are you going to the company Christmas party tomorrow night?" Greta asks changing the subject.

"No, I don't have the extra money and besides I need to be home with the kids until this thing with Todd passes over." Cheryl says while she takes a bit of her salad.

"You're going to miss a good old party. Plenty of booze and good food." Greta says as she rubs it in.

"That's your way of having a good time. I like to do things with my kids and tomorrow Ryan is taking us ice skating." Cheryl replies.

Cheryl finishes lunch and returns to work. Today she is working behind the customer service desk helping customers. With store being so busy the day flies by. Then as the clock nears three, she looks up and sees Gracie standing in line. Cheryl hopes the two people in front of her takes over five minutes, so she doesn't have wait on the old bat. The first customer just buys a book of stamps and the second one cashes in a five dollar scratch off lottery ticket. Cheryl gives the man the five dollar bill as Gracie walks up to the counter.

"How are my grandchildren?" Gracie says with a rude tone.

"They're doing good Gracie. How are you today?" Cheryl says with a fake smile.

"I'm fine, when are the kids coming over again?" Gracie asks loud and obnoxiously.

"I don't know. I can't jeopardize the children with Todd on the loose." Cheryl says.

"Well I have their Christmas gifts." Gracie says.

"Okay Gracie, you made your point what can I do for you?" Cheryl asks politely.

"I need a carton of Pall Mall non-filtered cigarettes." Gracie says.

"Here you go, that will be $87.75." Cheryl says as she puts the carton of cigarettes on the counter.

"The price of cigarettes is a rip off." Gracie says out loud and rudely.

"We don't make up the prices Mrs. LaRussa. The state has levied high taxes on these death sticks because of the sicknesses they cause." Greta says as she jumps into the conversation.

This shuts Gracie up as she takes her cigarettes and change from a one hundred dollar bill. Cheryl mouths the words thank you to Greta as she passes the customer service desk to punch out. Cheryl grabs her things from her locker and heads out the front door. She walks straight towards her car when a car viciously backs out of a parking space. Cheryl stops to avoid being hit by the car but the woman turns the wheel so the car heads right for her. Cheryl stands there in shock when all of a sudden she is pulled in-between two parked cars. Cheryl looks up and see the old man holding her by the shoulder.

"You really have to watch where you're going. Besides some people cannot drive very well." The old man says with a smile.

"Thank you," Cheryl says as she looks over at the person driving the car.

To her surprise, it's Gracie driving the car and not paying any attention to where she is going. She is oblivious to her surroundings when she is driving. Cheryl watches as Gracie drives off with a cigarette dangling out of her mouth. Before she leaves the parking lot she almost hits two more pedestrians.

"That woman is a menace to society and she shouldn't be driving." Cheryl says the old man.

There is no answer from the old man. Cheryl turns around and he is walking into the store. Cheryl smiles and doesn't chase after him. She makes her way to her car. She starts the car and turns on the radio. She pulls out of the parking lot and goes to pick up Danielle when she sees Todd standing on the corner. Cheryl pushes down on the accelerator and tears a patch of tread on the pavement. Todd gestures with his fingers, like he is shooting her with a gun. Cheryl drives as fast as she can to get away from him. When she gets to the next light she calls 911. She tells the dispatcher where Todd is located. Within a couple of minutes there are three squad cars in the vicinity but Todd is nowhere to be seen. Cheryl rushes to pick up both kids from school and from there she drives directly home. When Cheryl walks in the front door Ryan is busy working at the dining room table. Ryan hears them come in and he gets up to meet them at the front door. He can see the fear in Cheryl's eyes.

"What happened?" Ryan asks.

"That bastard Todd is still here. Now he is standing on corners gesturing a gun in his hands as he shoots me." Cheryl replies.

"Cheryl, relax your safe here with me. Look the sheriff's car is still here too." Ryan says trying to calm her down.

"We're not safe anywhere. Just to think I was living with him for fourteen years and not knowing what he is capable of. Get me a gun, please." Cheryl says in a rant.

"Calm down Cheryl, killing him isn't going to solve anything. Let the law take care of him." Ryan says as he grabs hold of Cheryl and holds her tight.

Cheryl calms down and grabs a glass of wine. She takes a long deep swig of wine when a delicious aroma overwhelms her senses.

"What the hell smells so good?" Cheryl asks.

"That would be my world famous roast beast as the Grinch would say." Ryan replies with the Grinch's evil smile.

"Roast beast huh, and what else has the chef mustered up?" Cheryl says pulling her long hair into pig tails like little Cindy Lou Who.

"That would be mashed potatoes, homemade gravy and corn." Ryan replies.

Cheryl smiles at Ryan's sense of humor. Cheryl and Ryan pick up all his books and clear off dining room table. Cheryl and Danielle set the dining room table when there is a knock on the door. Ryan goes to the door where one of the deputies is standing with Gracie. Ryan opens the door as Cheryl joins him.

"This woman claims to be your mother-in-law." The deputy says.

"She is, what do you want Gracie?" Cheryl asks.

"I stopped by to say I'm sorry for what Todd has done to you. I haven't treated you very well and I want to apologize for that also." Gracie says with her head down.

"What is this all about?" Ryan asks.

"Late this afternoon Todd threatened to kill me if I didn't give him some cash. The FBI has frozen all his bank accounts and he and his tramp are broke. I gave him what I had on me. He took off and I called the police on him. He is a bad egg and I will apologize again." Gracie says with tears dripping from her eyes.

"Why such a change of heart?" Ryan asks with a temper.

"Because it took that type of incident for me to realize that Cheryl and the kids are all I have." Gracie says with tears streaming down her face.

Cheryl smiles at the little old lady. She puts her arms out and hugs Gracie.

"Would you like to have dinner with us?" Cheryl asks.

"I would love too." Gracie responds.

Ryan stands there and looks at Cheryl in awe. He says to himself what just happened here. So they set an extra place setting at the table for Gracie. Everything is brought out on dishes and served family style. Before anyone takes a morsel of food Cheryl says grace. Everyone says amen when Cheryl finishes. Ryan made a six pound roast beef which was more than enough for the five people at the table. They even fix two dishes for the deputies sitting out in their car. When Gracie finishes her dinner she hugs everyone with the exception of Ryan. She puts her coat on and says good night as she heads home. Ryan and Cheryl clean the dishes off the dining room table after dinner. They laugh about Gracie and her change of heart. Ryan reiterates back to Cheryl that Gracie will be left alone after Todd is taken into custody. Soon the evening fades into bedtime. Everyone goes their own way with the exception of Ryan. He goes back to work on the case sitting at the dining room table. There is where he falls asleep with his face in a books.

Chapter 17 – Ice Skating Party

On Saturday morning, Cheryl comes down the stairs and she looks over at the couch. She sees the afghan still in place and Ryan is nowhere to be seen. She walks into the kitchen and starts to prepare coffee. She puts the water in the pot and starts to add the coffee, when she hears a rumbling sound coming from the dining room. Cheryl quietly walks in and see Ryan sleeping with his arms folded around his head. She takes out her camera and snaps a picture. Ryan hears the snap and sees the flash. He lifts his head slowly off the table and looks over at Cheryl.

"What time is it?" Ryan asks in a sleepy voice.

"It's ten minutes to eight." Cheryl replies with a smile.

"Oh shit you guys are going to be late for school and work." Ryan says as he gets up from the table in a rush.

"Slow down there big boy. It's Saturday." Cheryl responds with a big smile.

"Oh yeah, wow, I'm in another world." Ryan replies.

"Go wash up and I will make you breakfast. Remember you promised to take Danielle and I ice skating today?" Cheryl says with a devilish smile.

Ryan goes upstairs and jumps in the shower. He puts his head under the water and just sits there. The warm water feels good rolling over his head and down his face. After his shower, Ryan gets dressed and smells something good cooking. The aroma is sneaking up the stairs as he gallops down the stairs like a herd of elephants. Ryan walks into the kitchen wearing a pair of jeans and a sweatshirt. His bare feet are slapping against the hard wood floors as walks towards the stove.

"What smells so good?" Ryan asks as walks over to Cheryl standing in front of the stove.

"You see, you're not the only one that can cook. Grab a seat and I will serve up my famous French toast and sausage. How many pieces of French toast would you like?" Cheryl asks.

"Three pieces of French toast and three sausage links." Ryan says as pours himself a mug of hot coffee.

Within minutes of Ryan getting his breakfast, both Danielle and Michael are coming down the stairs. That distinct aroma of French toast in intoxicating. This is one of Cheryl's mom's recipes that no one else knows how to prepare. The kids grab a seat at the table and wait for their plates. Within a minute or two Cheryl comes in the dining room with three plates. One for Danielle, Ryan and one for Michael. Ryan sits at the table and gobbles down his breakfast in minutes.

"Where did you learn how to make this?" Ryan asks.

"Ancient Cheryl secret." Cheryl says to Ryan referring back to his comment a couple of days ago about the pancakes.

Danielle and Michael both laugh at their mom's comment. They pour the syrup over their French toast as Cheryl comes in with her own plate. Ryan gets up and grabs another cup of coffee and he sits back down at the table.

"This is how all meals should be." Danielle says to Ryan and Cheryl.

Cheryl and Ryan look at each other and smile.

"Are we ready for some ice skating today?" Ryan says.

"Sure am." Danielle says.

"Yes I am Cheryl I am." Cheryl replies in a Dr. Seuss phase.

"Not really, but I'll come along and play in the arcade if that's alright?" Michael says.

"I'm okay with that, how about you mom. What do you think?" Ryan says.

"Sounds good to me." Cheryl replies.

"Yes," Michael says with a fist pump.

By noon everyone is washed up and ready to go. Everyone is wearing heavy layers on this cold December morning because the rink is open to the elements. They make it out to the car and drive down to the local ice rink. Ryan pays the skating fees and the skate rentals. Michael hobbles into the arcade on his crutches. Ryan, Cheryl and Danielle put on their skates. They balance as the walk towards the rink on the rubber padding. Ryan is the first one on the ice. Danielle is second and Cheryl is third. Danielle picks it up quickly for she has been on skates many times before. Cheryl skates very well as she breezes by a struggling Ryan as he tries to balance. Ryan starts to swing both arms in a looping motion and falls backwards. He lands right on his butt. Ryan is quick to get back up and on his feet.

"I guess ice skating isn't your cup of tea." Cheryl says laughingly as she flies by Ryan.

"I thought you said you could skate?" Danielle says to Ryan.

Ryan looks at Danielle like he his hiding something. When Cheryl comes around to lap Ryan again he plays the awkward nerd that can't skate a lick. Cheryl laughs out loud as she passes him a second time.

"Shh," Ryan says to Danielle.

Ryan starts to move by putting one foot in front of the other. He picks up speed as he comes up to the first turn. Cheryl moves around the second turn and sees Danielle all by herself. Ryan is quickly moving up behind Cheryl skating like a pro. Cheryl on the other hand, looks around the rink wondering where Ryan went too. Before she can turn around Ryan grabs her around the hips and lifts her up and over his head. He turns around and skates in circles with her above his head. He looks up quickly at Cheryl and she has the biggest grin. Quickly, Ryan brings Cheryl back down and sets her on the ice.

"You had me going. I thought you couldn't skate a lick, you could skate all along." Cheryl says as they skate hand in hand.

"Nice move Ryan," Danielle says as she passes them on the inside.

Ryan just smiles and goes with the flow. The three skate for an hour and a half before they take a hot chocolate break. Michael comes out of the arcade to join them. Then back to the ice for another hour. Danielle watches Ryan and Cheryl as they skate together. They are talking and laughing the entire time they are together. It's like they were meant for each other. By three in the afternoon Ryan and Cheryl are spent. They decide that's it for the day as they all get off the ice. They switch out their skates in return for their shoes. They go into the arcade to get Michael and then head to the car.

"Mom, I want a white Christmas! Is it ever going to snow?" Michael asks.

"Michael I can't make it snow. If we're meant to have a white Christmas, it will snow." Cheryl replies.

"How about a steak dinner?" Ryan says changing the subject.

Cheryl, Danielle and Michael all say yes simultaneously. Ryan puts the car in gear and drives to Syracuse. He pulls into Delmonico's and the two kids start cheering because they have pestered Cheryl and Todd too many times to go there. They all order whatever they want to eat. Cheryl and Danielle get the New York Strip Steak. Michael is not much of a steak man so he orders a hamburger. Ryan goes with the best as he orders a twenty-four ounce Porterhouse Steak. Everyone is hungry from skating as they demolish their food. There are no leftovers and no doggie bags to take home.

"How about dessert?" Ryan asks.

"No, I couldn't eat another thing." Cheryl says.

"Sure," Michael replies with a grin.

"Can I have two molting Chocolate cakes with two scoops of vanilla ice cream?" Ryan tells the waitress.

When the desserts come out, there are two spoon for each dessert.

"Look at those desserts! They are huge." Danielle says.

Danielle and Michael share one dessert while Ryan and Cheryl share the other one. When they finish with their desserts they prepare to leave the restaurant. Both Cheryl and Ryan stand up and look at each other. The muscles in their legs are hurting from ice skating. Slowly they both get up as the lactic acid in their muscles start to stiffen and soreness settles in.

"I'm going to be a hurting unit tomorrow." Ryan says to Cheryl.

"Tell me about it. I am as stiff as a board right now." Cheryl replies.

The four exit the restaurant and get into the car as they head home. The night is clear and cold with just a few traces of snow on the ground.

"It doesn't even feel like Christmas time." Michael says as he puts his head against the window.

"How about we make Christmas cookies tomorrow?" Danielle asks.

"We can do that, I'm kind of craving the chocolate ones with the walnuts." Cheryl replies.

"Christmas cookies, wow I haven't had them since I was a kid and lived at home with my parents. Count me in!" Ryan says with a grin.

The forty-five minute ride home is fun because everyone is taking about what kind of cookies they are going to bake. When they get home everyone relaxes in the great room with a roaring fire and hot chocolate to warm everyone up. By nine thirty, Michael is sound asleep lying on Cheryl's shoulder. Danielle is fighting to keep her eyes open. Ryan picks Michael up and carries him to bed. Danielle follows Ryan and goes right to bed without an argument because she is exhausted. Ryan makes his way back downstairs with four Advil in hand. Two for himself and two for Cheryl. He grabs a large glass of water and takes his two Advil. He walks back into the great room where Cheryl is staring at the Christmas tree with tears in her eyes.

"Here, take these, they will help you feel better." Ryan says as he hands her the other two Advil.

"Thanks," Cheryl replies as she looks at Ryan.

"Hey, what's wrong?" Ryan says when he sees the tears in her eyes.

"We have a Christmas tree and I have just a few small items to put under the tree for the kids." Cheryl says as a stream of tears flows over her cheeks.

"Hey don't worry about that. I can help." Ryan replies as he sits next to her and wraps his arms around her.

"No Ryan, I can't accept that. You have done so much for us already." Cheryl says as she snuggles under Ryan's arm.

"I won't take no for answer. Tomorrow after we bake cookies and eat dinner, you and I will do some Christmas shopping for the kids." Ryan replies.

"I," Cheryl says as she is interrupted.

"It's settled there is no arguing. No kid should spend Christmas morning looking under a vacant tree." Ryan says as he strokes his hand through Cheryl's long auburn hair.

As the night moves on, Cheryl and Ryan sit together in each other's arms looking at the fire burning in the fireplace. There the two adults fall asleep in each other's arms.

Chapter 18 – Christmas Cookies

On Sunday morning, everyone has a hard time getting up and out of bed. Cheryl and Ryan react like a couple of old goats as they moan and groan and get up off the couch. They are sore and their muscles are stiff and that makes it hard for them to walk.

"Oh God, I have to start working out. I hurt in places I never thought I had muscles." Cheryl says as she hobbles to the bathroom.

Ryan laughs out loud as he hobbles into the kitchen to make some coffee. Cheryl gets the kids up and the four of them go to morning mass at St Anthony's. After mass ends at ten thirty, they stick around and eat breakfast. Then all four of them help prepare the stage located inside the school for the Christmas play. They all have a good time and enjoy each other's company. Cheryl is busy working on the costumes while Ryan and kids work on the props. Then out of the side of her eye Cheryl sees Father Angelo walking towards her. She swallows hard when he sits next to her.

"Good morning Cheryl, it's so nice to see you here and who is that young man with your kids." Father Angelo says putting Cheryl on the spot.

"It's not what you think Father. He is a friend and he is helping me and the children out tremendously." Cheryl replies.

"Oh no child I believe you. I can see how he is with your children. I can see love in his eyes when he is looking over at you." Father Angelo replies.

"He is so nice and goes out of his way for us. He treats us like Todd should have been doing over the years." Cheryl says.

"Where is Todd?" Father Angelo asks.

"I don't know but he has turned into pure evil." Cheryl says with tears welling in her eyes.

"I told you to have faith and God will see you struggling. He works in mysterious ways my child. He will protect you from whatever evil's out there stalking you. Mark my words Cheryl everything will work out." Father Angelo says as he gets up.

By one o'clock everyone is home and making Christmas cookies. The first batch is sugar cut out cookies. The second batch is Cheryl's favorite chocolate walnut cookies. By three o'clock the third batch of Italian cookies are being rolled out and baked.

"Is anyone hungry?" Ryan asks.

"I'm starved." Michael replies.

"I second that notion." Danielle says.

"What did you have in mind?" Cheryl asks.

"Well we have some left over pasta salad and macaroni salad. I was thinking Hoffman hotdogs grilled to perfection." Ryan says.

"Go for it Chef Emeril." Cheryl replies jokingly.

Ryan grabs six frozen Hoffman hotdogs out of the freezer. He goes out the backdoor through the mud room. The backdoor leads to a deck where the gas grill is located. Cheryl finishes up the last batch of cookies as she sets them on a cooling tray. Ryan comes back inside to get a platter for the grilled hotdogs. He grabs the platter as Cheryl starts washing all the bowls and trays from the cookies.

"Mom, can I have a cookie?" Michael asks.

"After dinner." Cheryl replies.

"Just one, I promise I will eat my dinner." Michael pleads.

"No cookies," Cheryl says loud and clear.

"Did someone say cookies, I love cookies." Ryan says as he walks into the kitchen wearing a cookie monster mask and talking like cookie monster.

"Where did you find that mask?' Cheryl asks while trying not to laugh out loud.

Both Danielle and Michael are in hysterics. Ryan bounces up and down as he walks towards the cookies.

"Cookie, cookie, cookie." Ryan says as he grabs for a cookie.

"I told them no and that goes for you too cookie monster." Cheryl says as she cracks Ryan on the butt with a wooden spoon.

"Cookie monster not happy." Ryan says as he walks out holding his butt.

"Don't ever mess with the cookie maker. Do you hear me cookies monster." Cheryl says while laughing.

Ryan goes out the back door wearing the cookie monster mask but returns without the mask. He is carrying the hotdogs on the platter.

"How did that feel Cookie Monster?" Cheryl says to Ryan.

"Cookie Monster, what are you talking about? Did I miss something here?" Ryan asks like an innocent bystander.

"I'll give you another crack across the butt." Cheryl says with the wooden spoon in hand.

"Okay Cookie Monster has had enough!" Ryan says with cookie monsters voice.

They all head to the dining room to eat dinner. Cheryl grabs the two salads and Danielle brings in the dishes and cutlery. Ryan sets the hotdogs on the table and goes back into the kitchen to get the condiments. Ryan returns and sets the ketchup and mustard on the table. He grabs his fork and looks for his two well-done hotdogs.

"Okay where are my hotdogs?" Ryan asks.

"Cookie Monster ate them." Cheryl says with cookie monsters voice.

"That's it I have had enough?" Ryan says as he gets up and walks away from the table looking angry.

"Where are you going?" Cheryl asks.

"I'm going to kill that Muppet. No one messes with my hotdogs." Ryan says

Cheryl, Danielle, and Michael bust out laughing. Cheryl is laughing so hard, she has a hard time putting Ryan's hotdogs back on the platter. All along Cheryl has the two well-done hotdogs on her fork and she was hiding them under the table. After Ryan's escapade they all sit at the dining room table talking about Christmas while eating dinner. After dinner Cheryl and Ryan clean up the dishes. By six o'clock they are heading out the door for some Christmas shopping. Danielle and Michael stay home with the sheriffs car parked in the drive way.

"Where too?" Ryan asks.

"Let's start at Walmart." Cheryl replies.

"What about the mall? Ryan asks as he pulls out of the driveway.

"Its Sunday the mall closes at six." Cheryl replies.

So they drive to Walmart where they buy a few things for the children. They buy Michael a few board games, a few toys, and some stocking stuffers. They buy Danielle some hair accessories, a DS, and some stocking stuffers. They even buy wrapping paper and bows.

"What about this new Xbox One for Michael?" Ryan asks.

"Absolutely not. That is way too expensive." Cheryl says as she grabs Ryan by the arm and pulls him away.

Then they drive to Marshall's and buy clothing for both kids. Buy the times they finish shopping they have spent over five hundred dollars. When they get back to the house it's almost ten o'clock. They put the children to bed because they have school in the morning. Cheryl quietly pulls out all her wrapping supplies and prepares to wrap. She spreads out all the gifts and counts the quantity of gifts and the amount spent on each child.

"Hey Ryan dear, could you please get me a glass of wine?" Cheryl asks.

"Sure," Ryan says as he walks into the kitchen.

When Ryan returns, Cheryl has already began wrapping the gifts. With the few small odds and ends she bought before, both children have twelve gifts apiece. The amount of money spent on each child was within a couple dollars of each other. Cheryl was happy with the end results and Ryan was just happy to sit on the couch with his feet up on the ottoman.

"We did good honey." Cheryl says to Ryan who is passing out.

"Huh, oh yea, yea we did." Ryan says like he is out of it.

Cheryl just smiles and doesn't say another word to Ryan. She finishes wrapping everything up and sets them under the tree. By midnight everything is done and cleaned up. Cheryl grabs an afghan and covers up the snoring Ryan. Then she heads up stairs and turns in for the night.

Chapter 19 – Monday December 15th

On Monday December 15th, Ryan finishes up his final preparation for the custody and divorce hearing scheduled for tomorrow. Ryan is hoping that Todd will be stupid enough to show his face because he will be arrested right there on the spot. Ryan also hopes that he doesn't show up because that will be a victory for Cheryl by default. Ryan continues to work on the dining room table because he refuses to leave the house empty for Todd to break in again.

Cheryl, on the other hand, takes the children to school and goes to work. She is still a little sore from Saturday's ice skating outing. Cheryl works diligently when a sheriff's deputy stops in at the store. He walks up to the desk as Cheryl waits on him.

"Hello deputy, tell me you got that SOB?" Cheryl asks

"No sorry to say we haven't but we are closing in on him. We did manage to catch his estranged girlfriend." The deputy responds.

"Where did you find her?" Cheryl asks.

"In some flea bag motel located on the south side of Syracuse." The deputy says with a grin.

"No sign of Todd though?" Cheryl asks.

"He can't go very far because we have all his belongings including their money. All Todd has is his car and what money he has on him." The deputy replies.

"Please get him because I'm scared for the well-being of my children." Cheryl pleads.

"We're working night and day. I'm hoping we get him soon for your family's sake." The deputy says as turns to leave.

"Thank you," Cheryl says as the deputy waves his hand up acknowledging her with his back facing her as he walks out of the store.

"What was that all about?" Greta asks.

"They apprehended Todd's girlfriend but he is still at large." Cheryl replies.

"Have faith my friend, it's almost over." Greta says.

"Yeah, but this scares me because Todd snaps when he is cornered. He will be violent and he will move on instinct. He will do things without thinking about the consequences." Cheryl says.

The day goes by quickly and soon Cheryl and Greta are leaving for the day. Cheryl still has a sheriff's car following her around town. Cheryl does her normal things picking up the kids after work and then going home. Greta gets into car and heads home to her apartment. When she gets there she is in for a surprise. She pulls out her apartment key to unlock the door when she feel a knife against her throat.

"Don't says a word or I will slit your throat. Get the door open" Todd says.

"Please don't hurt me." Greta pleads for her life.

"If you don't do as I say I will slit you throat right here and now." Todd says as pulls the knife with force against her neck.

Greta stumbles and fumbles nervously with her keys. She is shaking as she tries to put the key into the slot. On the third try she gets the key into the slot and opens the door. Todd pushes her inside the apartment. Greta trips and falls to the floor.

"Get up!" Todd yells at Greta as he closes the door behind him.

Greta slowly gets to her feet. She starts to rub her right shoulder because that part of her body took the initial hit on the hardwood floor in the foyer.

"Make me something to eat." Todd yells in an angered tone.

Greta doesn't say a word and walks slowly into her kitchenette. She pulls out a Styrofoam container of day old Chinese food. Todd grabs it out of her hand and starts eating the sweet and sour chicken out of the container. Greta looks at the desperate man while he eats like animal.

"Why don't you save yourself a lot of aggravation and turn yourself in. They may go lenient on you." Greta says as she tries to negotiate

"Mind your own business and make me a sandwich or something." Todd says as he eats with his hands.

Greta pulls out some lunch meat and mustard. She goes into the pantry and pulls out her loaf of American bread. She goes back to the counter and pulls out two slices of bread.

"Make me two sandwiches. One bologna and one ham. Smother both sandwiches with mustard." Todd says as he finishes the Chinese food.

Todd throws the foam container on the floor. He walks over to the refrigerator and opens it up. He looks around inside for something to drink. Greta looks over her shoulder at Todd as she makes the sandwiches.

"Do you have any beer?" Todd asks.

"I am a wine drinker but there may be one or two bottles of beer on the bottom shelf in the back." Greta says.

Todd rummages through the bottom shelf until he finds two bottles of Miller Beer. He grabs both bottles and pulls them out. He sets them on the counter and opens the first one. He lifts the bottle to his mouth and guzzles half of it.

"What do you want with me?" Greta asks.

"I will let you know in a few minutes." Todd says as he looks at his watch.

Greta finishes making the bologna sandwich. She hands it to Todd and he quickly takes a large bite out of the sandwich. He chews it very little and swallows it down with a blast of beer. Todd finishes the first sandwich in four bites. Greta then hands him the ham sandwich and he does the same.

"Make me one more of each for the road." Todd says

Greta uses up the rest of her lunch meat and makes Todd two more sandwiches. She puts both sandwiches into baggies and them into a plastic grocery bag. Todd finishes the first beer and opens the second.

"Now call Cheryl and tell her to come over here." Todd demands.

"I will do no such thing." Greta replies.

"You will do as I say." Todd says as he backhands Greta.

Greta falls backwards and slams her face into the corner of the counter. Greta loses her balance and falls to the floor. She slowly gets up and grabs her cheek. She pulls her hand away and her hand is covered in blood.

"Get up and call her." Todd yells in a demanding voice.

Greta slowly gets to her feet. She grabs the dish towel and applies pressure to the three inch gash just below her cheek bone.

"If you don't want any more you will call Cheryl right now." Todd says with harshness.

Todd throws Greta her pocketbook. With one hand on her face and the other hand rummaging through her purse, Greta continues to watch her capturer. When she finds her cell phone, she pulls it out of the pocket book. Greta looks at the screen of her phone as she looks for Cheryl's cell phone number.

"Come on, come on, quit playing and call her!" Todd yells in her face.

"I'm going as fast as I can." Greta says as she wastes time.

When Greta finds the number she hits dial. She slowly puts the phone up to ear and listens to the phone as it rings. The she hears Cheryl pick up the phone and before Cheryl can say hello, Greta says something to Todd. Greta holds the phone close to her ear so Todd cannot over hear what is transpiring on the other end.

"What do you want me to tell her?" Greta asks Todd loud and clear.

"Tell her you need her down here to help you with something." Todd says loud and clear.

Cheryl listens to the conversation on the other end. She knows Greta is in trouble and she needs to do something fast. Cheryl realizes Todd has becoming a madman and there is no stopping his crazy actions.

"Hi Cheryl, its Greta I was wondering if you could stop by later and help me with my hair. I'm trying a new color and I need your help." Greta says.

"Is that bastard there with you?" Cheryl whispers.

"Yes, yes you can bring the kids. I have a couple of gifts for them to put under the tree. When they get here they can also play my computer games" Greta says as she gives Cheryl a hint.

Todd waves for her to pull the phone away from her ear so he can listen to the conversation. Greta slowly pulls the phone away and sets it in the palm of her hand.

"That's great Greta, I will be happy to come down. I have to bring the groceries into the house first and then I'll be right down." Cheryl says as she plays along.

"Great Cheryl, I'll see you in a couple of minutes." Greta responds.

"Thanks, talk to you in a few." Cheryl says as she hangs up the phone.

"Good job, now take a seat." Todd says as he pushes Greta down into a kitchen chair.

Todd finishes the second bottle of beer. He goes back to the fridge and pulls out an open bottle of Merlot. Todd pulls out the cork and takes a deep long swig. Greta continues to apply pressure to the gash on her face.

"We got a few minutes before my lovely bride arrives. Take off your blouse." Todd says as he drinks from the wine bottle.

"You can stick it where the sun don't shine." Greta responds with attitude.

Todd walks over to Greta sitting at the table. He reaches for her blouse when Greta slaps his hand away. Todd lifts the wine bottle up and takes another long swig of wine. He sets the bottle down on the kitchen table while he pulls Greta to her feet. Greta tries to sit back down but Todd will not allow her. He grabs her button up blouse and rips it open. The buttons fly all over the kitchen floor. Greta tries to close up her blouse but Todd hold her hands back.

"Beautiful black lacy bra. I would never have thought you would be wearing such a sexy piece if lingerie. Do you have matching panties on?" Todd says as grabs hold of the button on her blue jeans.

"Would you really like to see?" Greta says playing along

Greta pulls back her free arm and puts it up on his shoulder. With one hand on his shoulder and the other one holding the dish towel on her face, Todd reaches for the button on her jeans. With one hand he pushes the button through the loop. Todd looks at Greta's face and sees the biggest smile on it.

"It looks like someone is enjoying themselves." Todd says with a dirty grin.

"Not as much as you." Greta says as she kicks him squarely with force in the balls. His knife falls to the floor and slides under the table.

Todd falls to the ground holding his private area as Greta makes a mad dash for the door. Todd reaches for Greta and gets a hold of one of her ankles. Greta trips and falls to the floor but manages to break free from Todd's grip. She treads with both hands and feet until she can get back up and run. She runs towards the door with her blouse undone yelling and screaming for help. When she reaches the door she tries to open it but it's locked. Greta undoes the lock and tries to pulls the door but Todd has latched the chain lock on top of the door. She quickly pulls the chain off the door and turns the handle and pulls the door open. Greta runs outside without even looking behind her. She runs off the small landing and towards the road. She sees the police cruisers driving up to her apartment with their lights on but sirens off.

Back inside Todd is slow getting up from the kick in the privates. He grabs his knife and gets to his feet. He staggers from side to side as he tries to regain his composure. He walks towards the door and see the sheriffs cruisers moving in on the apartment.

"Dam it." Todd says in disgust.

Todd closes the door, locks it and runs towards the back window. He opens the window, climbs out and runs into the darkness unseen. Greta is helped by the police where she is rushed to the hospital. The laceration is so deep, she gets ten stitches in her cheek. Cheryl arrives at the hospital while the doctor is stitching Greta's gash. Cheryl takes a seat at her best friend's side.

"Thanks for the heads up." Cheryl says as she hugs Greta.

"Thanks for calling the police. I thought for sure he was going to kill me" Greta replies.

The police tell Greta that's it's not safe to stay at home for the next few days. So she gathers a few things and moves in with Cheryl, Ryan and the kids. When they get to the house, Ryan had already ordered a couple of pizzas. Greta and Cheryl take a seat in the great room and eat their pizza. The girls get comfortable because Ryan has a roaring fire going in the fireplace.

"I can't wait to get this whole thing over with. Todd is out of control and he is making everyone's life miserable." Ryan says.

"It starts tomorrow when he loses complete custody of the children. Ryan make it happen." Greta says as she hold an ice pack on her badly bruised and stitched up face.

By ten o'clock the kids and the women are in bed. Greta is sharing the master bedroom with Cheryl. Ryan is still sleeping on the couch in the great room and the sheriff's car is still parked in the driveway. Greta takes a few pain killers and falls asleep quickly because she feels safe and secure with the amount of people inside and outside of the house.

Chapter 20 – The Court Date

The next day, Greta takes the kids to school. After she drops them off at school she goes to work. Ryan and Cheryl get up early and prepare for court. At nine o'clock they drive to county court for the custody hearing. The court time is set for ten in the morning. Cheryl and Ryan are ready at nine-thirty as they wait for the judge. At nine fifty-five the judge walks into the conference room and takes a seat at the head of the table. He sits down and opens a file and starts to read to himself. The judge doesn't say a word while he skims over the pages. Cheryl looks over at the judge as he reads. The judge doesn't make eye contact with neither Ryan nor Cheryl. When the hearing starts it was just like Ryan anticipated, Todd and his lawyer were no shows. Ryan grins knowing he came well prepared and ready for battle.

"Where is the plaintiff in this custody hearing?" The judge asks.

"Your honor, I don't think he will be arriving any time soon. He is wanted and on the run from the police." Ryan replies.

"Are you telling me this man is a felon and wants custody of two minors?" The judge says as he closes the file in front of him.

"I'm just giving you the facts your honor." Ryan replies.

"The plaintiff and his lawyer are a no show in my courtroom. My time is to valuable counselor. What do you have?" The judge asks.

If Ryan plays all his cards right he will win the case hands down. Ryan makes sure he includes all the incidents that Todd has been involved in over the past three weeks. He goes over the financial records and how Todd left Cheryl absolutely nothing. Ryan informs the judge that Todd's new pregnant girlfriend has been taken into custody by the police. The judge listens to everything Ryan has to say. Ryan takes up over an hour pleading Cheryl's case to the judge.

"I am going to take an hour recess to go over all the facts. This hearing is adjourned until twelve thirty. At that point, I will have my ruling on this case." The judge says as he gets up and takes the file off the table and goes into his chambers.

"How come he didn't make a decision right here and now?" Cheryl asks as the door closes behind the judge.

"He is just going to go over all the facts before he makes a decision." Ryan replies as he closes his portfolio.

"What are we going to do for the next hour?" Cheryl asks as Ryan as he puts his portfolio into his briefcase.

"Eat lunch of course." Ryan says as he puts on his long trench coat.

Ryan helps Cheryl with her coat as they make their way out of the courthouse. Ryan looks at his watch to make sure they have enough time to eat lunch and make it back before the judge returns. They hustle across the street to a local restaurant. When they get inside they take their coats off and grab a table in the back. Ryan is dressed in a gray pin stripe suit. Cheryl is wearing a white blouse with a black skirt.

"We need to order quickly and eat up. We don't want to be late when the judge returns from his chambers." Ryan says.

The waitress comes to the table and they order their beverages and lunch at the same time. Ryan orders a burger and fries and Cheryl order an antipasto. Their lunch arrives in record time and they start to eat. At one point, Cheryl looks up at Ryan and he is staring at her.

"What," Cheryl asks.

"Nothing, just looking at a beautiful woman sitting across from me." Ryan says with a smile.

"Hey, hey I'm your client." Cheryl says in a humorous tone.

"Not after today." Ryan says as they both break out in laughter.

They both finish their lunch and make it back to the courthouse with five minutes to spare. They go back into the conference room and sit in the same seats they were in earlier. At twelve thirty on the nose the judge reenters the room. He takes his seat at the head of the table and opens the file. The room is completely silent as Ryan and Cheryl wait for the verdict. After three minutes of silence the judge looks up at Cheryl and Ryan.

"With all the evidence that has been presented to me I have made up my decision. Cheryl you have proven your ability to be a very good mother. You have put their needs in front of your own. Any good parent makes sure their children are in a well-rounded home with good food on the table. With my judgment I rule in favor and I'm giving you full custody of your children. As for these divorce papers I will grant you the divorce from Todd if you like." The judge says with confidence.

"What about all the stipulations that Todd's lawyer incorporated in the divorce papers?" Cheryl asks.

"The only thing I'm granting from these divorce papers is the divorce. He gets nothing that he is asking for. It sound like to me, your ex-husband had been preparing for this divorce for some time. His actions tell me that he is immature and doesn't put his children's needs in front of his own. Todd will need to be evaluated before he gets any type of visitation rights." The judge states.

"Your honor what about the money Todd took from their joint savings account?" Ryan asks.

"Ryan that is out of my control at this point. Todd's accounts have been frozen and until everything is settled. That money will remain frozen until Todd is taken in to custody and tried." The judge says.

"Thank you your honor." Cheryl says.

"Good luck to you young lady. I hope everything falls in place for you. You seem like a very loving person. Your children are lucky to have you." The judge says as he gets up and leaves the room.

Cheryl jumps out of her seat and wraps her arms around Ryan with joy.

"Oh my god, I don't know how to thank you." Cheryl says with tears of joy streaming down her face.

"How about going out on a date with me?" Ryan replies as he hugs her tight.

"I'm not a divorced woman yet?" Cheryl says as she wipes the tears from her face.

"What, the judge just agreed to your divorce." Ryan says in seriousness.

"Yes I know but the papers are not filed yet. Maybe by the time we get home the papers will be filed. Just kidding, yes I would love to go out on a date with you." Cheryl replies as she hugs Ryan again.

Ryan packs up all his paperwork as they head out of the court house victorious.

"How do you want to celebrate your victory?" Ryan asks as they head out to the car.

"I would like to celebrate by cooking a porterhouse steak dinner for you and me." Cheryl says as they walk together arm in arm.

"What about the kids and Greta?" Ryan asks with sarcasm.

"We'll get them hot dogs!" Cheryl replies with a laugh.

"You're going to eat a steak while the kids and Greta eat a hotdog?" Ryan says while laughing out loud.

"Just sarcasm honey, I would never do that to my kids. Todd might, but I won't." Cheryl replies.

"Did you just call me honey?" Ryan asks.

"Yes I did." Cheryl says as she gives Ryan a kiss on the cheek.

Ryan opens the door for Cheryl and she gets into his car. Ryan walks around to the driver's side and opens his door. He puts his briefcase in the backseat and then he gets into the driver's seat. Ryan starts the car and drives off towards the grocery store.

In the alley way across the street from the court house Todd looks at Ryan and Cheryl. Todd makes sure he is far enough back in the alley so no one will see him. His temper flairs when he sees Ryan arm in arm with his now ex-wife. Todd kicks a garbage can in frustration in the alley as Ryan's car drives off. Todd is now on his own and on foot. His mother has disowned him for his actions and his girlfriend is in police custody. Todd left his car near Greta's apartment during the attack and it has been impounded. Todd doesn't have much money to survive on and he is running on instinct. Todd is in awe because everything that was going in his favor is spiraling out of control. Now the tides have been turned and he is on the run.

"You know the saying, a desperate man will do whatever it takes to survive." Todd says as he walks deeper into the alley to hide.

Chapter 21 – Wednesday December 17th

On the morning of Wednesday December 17th, everyone is up early getting ready for school and work. Greta is still staying at the house with Cheryl and her family because Todd is still at large. While everyone is getting dressed, Ryan makes breakfast for everyone. To keep everyone safe, Ryan drives everyone to their daily destination. When the last passenger Michael is dropped off at school, Ryan heads to Syracuse to work for a few hours.

Meanwhile Todd is working on his final plan. He is distraught over the situation. He is planning on creating a chaotic and dangerous situation for Cheryl and the children. Todd thinks about a vulnerable time for Cheryl and the kids as he sits in a diner across the street from Boyd's. He watches as Cheryl and Greta get out of Ryan's car and go inside the store.

"Happy go lucky, you wait and see what I have in store for you." Todd says as he sips his coffee.

"Hello there, can I take a seat here?" The old man says as he sits in the same booth as Todd.

Todd looks around the diner and sees it's almost completely empty. The old man sits across from Todd obstructing his view of the store.

"Why don't you sit somewhere else old man. The diner is practically empty and there are seats everywhere." Todd says in a loud crude voice.

"No, I want to sit here and talk to you." The old man states.

"Well, I don't want you to sit here with me." Todd says as he tries to get up.

"Sit down or else." The old man says a calm firm voice.

"Or else what? I don't see you stopping me from doing anything." Todd says as he slides out of the booth.

"Do you see that man sitting at the other end of the counter?" The old man says in a stern voice.

Todd looks up and across the counter. There is a well-dressed man drinking his coffee and eating his eggs. The well-dressed man looks up at Todd and makes eye contact. This makes Todd a little nervous of the situation.

"Yes I see him, why," Todd says standing at the side of his booth.

"He is a detective and all I have to do is yell out to him." The old man says.

Todd humbly sits back down into the booth. He slides across the bench seat and stares at the old man.

"Okay, you have my attention." Todd says.

"I am going to give you one opportunity to make this right. You had your chance with Cheryl and you threw it away. She is a loving mother that will do anything for her children. Unlike someone else I know. She will even die for her children in the wake of protecting them. You need to walk away from this situation or something bad is going to happen. Better yet, walk over to that detective and give yourself up." The old man says to Todd.

"What do you know?" Todd says while raising his voice.

"I know a lot more than you think." The old man replies.

"Really Mr Know It All. Tell me where I will be over the next ten years." Todd says with an attitude.

"Prison," The old man replies.

At that point Todd sees something in the old man's eyes. He turns around to look at the detective. Todd wants to make sure the old man didn't tip off the detective. Todd can see the detective still sitting with his head down and lifting his coffee cup to his mouth. Todd turns his head back to the old man.

"Good try old man, hey where did you go." Todd says as he looks around for the old man.

Todd looks under the booth for the old man that has suddenly disappeared. He walks to the bathroom that is located to the left of his booth. He walks inside to an empty bathroom. Todd walks back to his booth scratching his head.

"Did you lose something sir?" The waitress asks.

"Did you see where the little old man went?" Todd replies.

"I don't know sir, would you like some more coffee?" The waitress asks with the coffee pot in hand.

"Yes, are you sure you didn't see where he went?" Todd asks.

The waitress doesn't answer Todd and pours the coffee in his cup. Todd looks around the diner wondering where the old man went. Todd sits and wonders if he is cracking up or losing his mind. After a few minutes of pondering his sanity, Todd pays up and leaves the diner. He makes his way to an old abandoned building on the west side of the river. When he arrives at the building he looks in all directions before entering. Todd wants to make sure no one sees him when he enters the building. He pushes the plywood covered door off to the side and walks in. The building is old and musty smelling with water leaking in everywhere. Todd walks through a half an inch of water lying on the floor. He finds the staircase and walks up the concrete steps towards and old office overseeing the once thriving textile plant. In the office, there is a few old and broken office chairs, one desk with a broken leg on one side, and a dirty old mattress that Todd sleeps on. Todd lies down on the mattress with his hands behind his head. He listens to the water dripping in through the roof and spattering on the concrete floor below. Then all of a sudden his disposable cell phone rings. Todd looks at the screen and notices it's a local call coming in. He doesn't recognize the number and he is hesitant to answer it. Using bad judgment he answers it anyway.

"Hello," Todd says in a low discrete voice.

"Todd, you have to get me out of here." Prudence says.

"What are you stupid, I told you not to call me." Todd replies in disgust.

"If you don't bail me out I'm going to tell them where your hiding." She says.

"Go right ahead, you really are an air head." Todd says as he hangs up on the call.

Todd quickly takes the battery out of the cell phone so the police cannot track the signal. He is not concerned that his girlfriend will tell them where he is hiding. Todd knows how to play the game. He moved out of his old hiding place and found a new one after Prudence was captured. Todd isn't nervous or overwhelmed as he lights up a Marlboro cigarette and inhales it deeply. He crosses his legs and relaxes on the mattress.

"All woman are stupid. I don't know how I fell for her." Todd says as he takes a deep drag off his cigarette.

Todd finishes his cigarette and crushed the butt out on the floor. He pulls up an old wool army blanket and covers himself. He thinks to himself and trances into a deep thought pattern on his next move.

"I will bring that bitch to justice." Todd says referring to Cheryl. "No one gets the best of Todd LaRussa."

Todd thinks of ways to get to Cheryl and the kids. He tries to figure out how he can get close to her without being seen and kill her. He is still set on kidnapping the children and taking them away. Over and over he plays scenarios out in his head. Every time there is something that messes up the plan. Within an hour of playing war games in his head, Todd passes out.

By the end of the day Cheryl, Greta and the children are safe and secure as they turn the car into the driveway. When they arrive at the house the sheriff's car is still waiting in the driveway. Ryan pulls up alongside and asks them if there has been any sign of Todd. The deputy in the passenger side replies they haven't seen or heard anything. They even took turns walking around the house and there is no sign of anyone. Ryan rolls up the window and continues up the driveway where he drops Cheryl, Greta and the children off at the front porch. They walk up the stairs and go into the house. Ryan parks the car in the garage. Then he does a quick inspection for himself as he walks around the house before it gets dark. During the month of December it gets dark by four thirty in the northeast. As Ryan walks around the house he checks all the windows and doors to make sure they are locked. He looks down at the muddy ground for footsteps coming from the back field or from a neighbor's house. When Ryan is satisfied with the walk around, he goes into the house. There he is greeted by Cheryl.

"Here you go grill master." Cheryl says as she hands him a platter of hamburger patties and matches.

"You know you got that right. At least I don't burn them." Ryan says in a laughing tone.

"Don't even go there if you know what's good for you." Cheryl says sarcastically.

Ryan takes the burgers and goes out on the back deck. He lights the grill and waits for it to heat. When it's hot enough he throws the burgers on the grill. He knows he is missing something that he always has every time he grills. He turns to walk back inside the house where he is met by Cheryl.

"I though you would need this." Cheryl says as she hands him a bottle of Labatt's Blue beer.

"You are a life saver." Ryan says as he takes the beer and kisses her gently on the lips.

Cheryl goes back into the house. Ryan grills the burgers and drinks his beer. He looks off his deck and watches the orange glow from the sun as it sets. Even though it's late fall the weather feels like winter. Ryan can see his breath as he breathes out. The temperatures outside are cold and hover around twenty degrees. Ryan finishes the burgers and takes them off the grill. He puts them on a clean platter. Ryan closes the grill and looks into the field behind the house. He thinks he sees something moving against the darkening sky. Ryan tries to focus on the image but it's getting to dark to see.

"It's probably a deer." Ryan says as he goes into the house.

Ryan locks the door behind him and shuts off the deck light. He makes his way into the dining room where Cheryl and Greta have set the table. They all take a seat and eat the meal together. Later that evening they light a fire in the fireplace and eat ice cream sundaes while watching *Rudolph the Red Nose Reindeer* follow by *Frosty the Snowman*. By ten pm everyone is in bed with the exception of Cheryl and Ryan. Cheryl has just finished cleaning up the kitchen and starts the dish washer. Ryan is getting the couch ready for bed as he grabs a handgun from his briefcase and tucks it under his pillow.

"What was that?" Cheryl asks Ryan catching him by surprise.

"It's a handgun for our safety." Ryan replies.

"Do you really think a gun is necessary?" Cheryl states to Ryan with her hands on her hips.

"Yes, I thought I saw someone moving out in the field tonight. I want to make sure if he gets in here, he leaves in a body bag." Ryan says.

"Ryan I am not comfortable with a gun in the house especially with a curious eight year old." Cheryl replies in a worried tone.

"I will make sure it's put away in the morning." Ryan states as he lies down on the couch.

"No, you will put it away now for everyone's safety." Cheryl say as she stares a hole through Ryan.

Ryan lays on the couch thinking Cheryl will just go to bed. Ryan closes his eyes and waits for her to walk away, but she just stands there waiting patiently for Ryan to do the right thing.

"Okay, you win." Ryan says as he gets up and grabs the handgun.

He walks over to his briefcase and puts the handgun inside. He uses the key on his keychain to lock the briefcase. From there, Ryan walks over to the closet and sets the briefcase on the top shelf.

"Are you happy now?" Ryan says as he walks back to the couch.

"Thank you, but you can have this if he breaks in during the night." Cheryl replies as she hands him his baseball bat.

"I can do just as much damage with this as I can with a handgun." Ryan says as he takes the bat out of her hand.

"I have faith you and I believe you will only injure him." Cheryl says as she gives Ryan a big hug.

Cheryl heads up the stairs to bed. Ryan lays awake staring at the ceiling thinking of the image he saw in the field. He has a restless night as he listens to every little sound and creak that the night has to offer.

Chapter 22 – Too Close for Comfort

The next morning Thursday December 18th, everyone is up to the smell of bacon cooking. Ryan had a hard time sleeping so he decided to get up early and make everyone breakfast. Cheryl is the first one downstairs as she pours herself a cup of coffee.

"What's all this for?" Cheryl asks.

"I couldn't sleep last night so I decided to get up early and make breakfast." Ryan replies.

"Oh my god, I can smell that upstairs." Danielle says as she comes running in the kitchen.

Ryan cooks up a pound of bacon, twelve eggs, and a half a loaf of bread for toast. Everyone sits down at the dining room table and digs in. Fifteen minutes later, everything is completely wiped out. Danielle and Greta clean off the table while Cheryl unloads and reloads the dishwasher. After breakfast Ryan takes the children to school. From there he drives to Syracuse to work one last time before the holidays. Cheryl and Greta drive to work together in Cheryl's car.

The work and school day goes by fast. As the clock approaches two thirty in the afternoon, Danielle is outside the middle school waiting for Cheryl to pick her up. Cheryl on the other hand, is running a little late because Greta is being held up by a disgruntled customer.

"Do you need a ride?" Makala asks Danielle

Makala and Danielle are school mates and have been friends since kindergarten.

"No, my mom should be here anytime, but thanks anyway." Danielle replies.

Danielle waits and waits while all the children slowly disappear from the front of the school. By two forty-five Danielle is alone and by herself when she sees a man walking from the road. Danielle turns and runs back towards the school. Every couple of seconds Danielle turns and looks at the man and now he is running towards her. When Danielle reaches the school she pulls on the door and it's locked from the inside.

"Open the door, please open the door." Danielle yells frantically.

"Danielle, stop I'm not going to hurt you." Todd yells as he runs towards her.

Danielle continues to pull on the door in a panicked state. She continues to yell out loud as Todd is quickly approaching her. Even though he is her father, she is frightened of him. He has changed from an unloving father into a crazed lunatic. All Danielle can see in her mind is the scars and injuries on Greta and her mother. She knows what her father is capable of and she doesn't want to become another victim.

"Please, please someone open the door." Danielle yells in a panicked state.

Danielle turns around and Todd is running up the front stairs. Todd is closing the gap as Danielle pulls the locked door in a frenzy to get it open.

"You bitch, how you dare run away from me." Todd yells as he grabs her on the upper arm.

Danielle screams at the top of lungs as Todd pulls her toward him. Danielle reacts by swinging her school bag at Todd. She hits him square in the face knocking him backwards. Todd falls backwards and loses his balance on the top step. He falls down onto the five concrete stairs bashing his head against the pointed corner of the second step. Todd hits so hard he cuts a deep wedge into his forehead just above his right eyebrow. Todd is slow to get up as he tries to get his bearings. As Todd manages to get up, he is a little weary from the gash on his head. The deep gash is there, but there is no blood coming out of the wound. Danielle looks at Todd as he shakes his head from side to side as he tries to get his bearings. Then Danielle hears the door unlatch and open behind her.

"Miss, are you alright?" Mrs. Cartwright, the principle, asks.

Danielle slowly walks backwards towards the open door never taking her eyes off Todd. Todd watches as Danielle reaches for the door while still looking at him. Todd reaches up to his forehead when he starts to feel something dripping on his cheek. Todd puts his hand over the deep gash when blood starts to flow through his fingers. Danielle turns and runs towards the open door.

"Call 911 Mrs. Cartwright." Danielle screams as she rushes inside the door.

Mrs. Cartwright takes out her cell phone and dials 911. Todd can't hold the wound closed as blood spills from his forehead like a stream. Todd runs up to the stairs and pulls on the door but it is locked upon being closed.

"Let me in, let me in or I will kill you!" Todd yells in a rampage.

Mrs. Cartwright explains to the 911 operator of the deranged man outside the school. He is yelling, screaming and threating the life of a child. Danielle walks back towards the wall and falls to the floor crying out loud while her father acts like a madman. Mrs. Cartwright looks on in horror as Todd punches a glass panel in the door. The glass doesn't break because the school had safety glass installed. Danielle kicks her feet and pushes herself into a corner. Mrs. Cartwright sits down and puts her arm around Danielle to console her. Todd continues to try and punch a hole through the window. On the forth try he breaks two knuckles on his right hand. He pulls his hand away in pain.

"You'll be alright Danielle. He can't get you in here." Mrs. Cartwright says to Danielle.

Within two or three minutes a few teachers start gathering by the front door. Todd looks inside and sees five or six teachers at Danielle's side. Then he hears the siren and makes a run for it. Todd darts around the side of the school and then runs towards the back. Todd runs at full speed until he sees the ten foot fence in front of him. There he leaps half way up and vigorously climbs up and over the fence. Todd moves towards the nature trail and disappears into the heavy dense wooded area.

When the police arrive, Todd is running deep into the nature trail. The police call it in and beef up security in the area as they search for him. One of the police officers goes into the school and starts to talk to Danielle. She is traumatized over the situation and she is crying out of control. That is when Cheryl and Greta arrive. Cheryl runs up the stairs and sees a pool of blood as she begins to panic. She runs up the stairs and starts banging on the door.

"Danielle, Danielle are you alright?' Cheryl yells out loud.

One of the teachers open the door and lets her and Greta in. Cheryl sees her daughter sitting on the floor crying. She runs over to her and wraps her arms around her.

"Are you alright baby?" Cheryl asks.

"I want to go home, I want to go home." Danielle cries out.

"Oh my God, I'm just a few minutes late and that bastard almost abducts my baby." Cheryl says as she cries in relief that her daughter is alright.

Cheryl helps Danielle to her feet and holds the frightened girl. They start to head towards the door when a police officer stops them.

"I still need to ask her a few more questions." The officer asks.

"No, I'm taking her home." Cheryl replies.

"I really need to ask her for a description of the perp." The officer says with a tight grip on Cheryl's arm.

"Get your hands off me. You have a description of my ex-husband. Now get your ass out there and find him before any more harm comes to my family." Cheryl says as she shrugs his hand off her arm.

Cheryl and Greta both walk towards their car with Danielle between them. Cheryl sits in the backseat with Danielle while Greta drives. Their next stop is the elementary school to pick up Michael. Michael on the other hand is off the crutches but still walks with a limp. After they pick him up, they race home and the lock all the doors. The girls sit in the great room traumatized from Todd's actions. They sit in the darkness with the exception of the Christmas tree lights. Greta decides to light a fire in the fireplace while Michael watches cartoons on the TV. Danielle decides to take a long hot shower to relax and then she joins everyone in the great room. By six in the evening Ryan makes it home from the office. Everyone is sitting so quietly on the couches and this is concerning to Ryan.

"Did I miss something?" Ryan asks.

"Yea, Danielle was almost abducted by Todd today." Cheryl replies.

"What happened?" Ryan asks.

"Greta and I were running late from work and Todd tried to kidnap her from the front of the school. She was able to get back inside the school but it was close call." Cheryl says with tears forming in her eyes.

"Are you alright Danielle?" Ryan asks as he goes over and hugs her.

Danielle is filled with emotion and begins to cry in Ryan's arms.

"It was so horrible. The way he came after me and the tone of his voice." Danielle says with tears streaming down her face.

"Today was my last day of work until after the new year. Tomorrow is the kids last day of school until Monday January 5th. I will stay with the kids night and day or until Todd is taken into custody." Ryan states.

Ryan goes into the kitchen and see everyone was too upset to make dinner. So Ryan takes out his cell phone and orders a party platter of pizza and wings for dinner. He grabs his bag and goes into the bathroom. He takes off his work suit and puts on his Syracuse University lazy pants with a big bulky sweatshirt. He grabs a beer out of the fridge and takes a seat next to Michael on the couch.

"Mom, what's for dinner? I'm starving." Michael asks.

"Michael, I'm not in the mood to cook. It's fend for yourself Thursday." Cheryl replies as she takes a small sip of wine.

"No it's not. Its pizza and wings Thursday." Ryan says as he tickles Michael.

When the pizza and wings arrive, Ryan meets the guy at the door. He pays the delivery man and sets the food on the coffee table in the great room. Greta goes into the kitchen and grabs plates and napkins. Then everyone digs in. It makes a happy ending for a day that could been devastating.

Chapter 23 – The Last Day of School

On Friday December 19^{th,} Ryan keeps his promise. He takes the kids to school while Cheryl and Greta ride to work together. He drops off the Michael and then he goes out to do a little Christmas shopping for the kids. He buys Michael and Danielle an expensive gift apiece and few other things. When he finishes with gifts for the kids, Ryan buys a few more gifts for Cheryl. The last gift he buys is a family gift that each and every one could share and enjoy.

"Now can I pick this gift up on Christmas Eve?" Ryan asks the clerk.

"Yes but we close at six pm, so be here before that." The clerk replies.

Ryan pays for the final gift and then goes to the house to wrap up all the gifts he bought. He does a pretty good job wrapping but it's not his forte. He tags all the gift to the kids from Mom and Ryan. The gifts for Cheryl are marked from Ryan and one each from the children. After Ryan is done wrapping the gifts he hides the gifts in the basement.

"I am getting so excited about Christmas. All we need is some snow and Christmas cheer." Ryan says as he hides the gifts inside old storage boxes in the basement.

On his way back up the stairs from the basement, Ryan is whistling *Jungle Bells*. He goes into the kitchen and grabs a bite to eat. When he walks into the great room he looks around.

"We need to decorate this entire room." Ryan says as he eats a sandwich.

After Ryan finishes his sandwich he goes into the attic and finds all the decorations. Box by box he brings everything down and into the great room. He decorates around the fireplace with more lights and garland. He puts out candles and Christmas décor upon on the all the tables. He runs a sting of lights and garland on the handrail going up the stairwell. He puts more stuff in the kitchen. He even puts out a beautiful candle decoration on the dining room table. Then he goes on the front porch and decorates around the front door with more light and garland. He even puts the icicle lights around the roof eave of the front porch. Then he puts a few lawn decorations out. One is Santa Claus and the other is a nativity scene.

"Eat your heart out Clark W Griswold." Ryan says as he attaches all the cords.

Ryan intertwines all the electrical cords together and puts them on a timer. He is so excited for Christmas because the last time he really enjoyed Christmas was when he was a kid. This is just a thirty-four year old acting like a fourteen year old. He tests the lights to make sure nothing is loose and all the lights are shining brightly. With all the lights on he looks over towards the two deputies sitting in the car. Ryan gives them a thumbs up and they both nod their heads up and down affirming that it looks good. Upon completion Ryan looks at his watch and sees it's almost two o'clock.

"Oh shit, got to get moving and get everything put away. Then it's off to go pick up Danielle." Ryan says as he gathers everything left over on the lawn.

Ryan quickly puts everything in the boxes and puts them back in the attic. He runs out the door and jumps into his car. He races to the middle school to pick up Danielle and then he goes and gets Michael. He keeps both of them away from the house by taking them shopping and then to the arcade at the mall. By five o'clock both Cheryl and Greta are getting out of work. Ryan makes sure he goes to Boyd's and waits for them to walk out the door. He watches as the two women walk towards Cheryl's car.

"What are we doing here?" Michael asks.

"We are going to follow your mom and Greta back to the house." Ryan replies with a grin.

"Why?" Danielle says with a look of concern on her face.

"Why do you ask, you will have to find that out when we get home." Ryan says with flair.

"Oh God, now what." Danielle says.

Ryan watches the two women get into the car and start heading towards the house on West Lake Rd. He keeps his distance as he keeps looking at the clock on the dashboard. Danielle notices Ryan is clock watching.

"Come on, come on." Ryan says as he waits for a light to change.

They drive back to the house and it feels like it takes forever. Ryan is filled with anticipation as the lights will turn on right at five-twenty. He looks at the clock and sees it's already five-eighteen.

"They're already going to be on when we get there." Ryan says to himself but loud enough for Danielle to hear him.

"What's going to be on, when we get where?" Danielle asks Ryan.

"You will see when we get there." Ryan answers as he keeps looking at the clock.

Danielle shakes her head in despair. The clock turns five-twenty and they still have a quarter mile to go. Ryan continues to look at the clock knowing he might have a few seconds to spare. Then they slow down and turn into the driveway. Ryan has his finger crossed and he figures everything will be lit as they come around the bend in the driveway. To his surprise they come around the bend and pass the sheriffs car in the darkness. Cheryl parks her car and Ryan parks right next to her. They get out of the car and all of a sudden its bright as day on the front lawn. Everyone's heads turn towards the Christmas light display on the front porch and yard.

"Merry Christmas to all, and to all a bright night." Ryan says full of cheer

"Wow, look at that." Michael says as he runs towards the front of the house.

"Oh my God, Ryan it's beautiful." Greta says.

"That is totally spectacular. It is amazing." Danielle says with a smile.

Cheryl turns towards Ryan and give him a big hug.

"You didn't have to do this." Cheryl says to Ryan.

"Yes I did. I want to make this a special Christmas for you and the kids." Ryan replies.

"It's absolutely beautiful, I don't know who is the bigger kid, you or Michael." Cheryl says to Ryan as they walk towards the front of the house with an arm around each other.

Ryan unlocks the front door and pushes it open. Cheryl walks in just behind him and when she turns on the light switch and all the Christmas decorations turn on inside the house. The interior of the house has a Christmas aura with the soft light emanating throughout.

"Oh my god," Cheryl says as she walks into the great room.

"This must have taken you all day to do?" Danielle asks.

"All we need is a fire and I will be in the Christmas spirit." Greta says.

They start up a fire in the fireplace and drink a hot cup of chocolate. Ryan preheats the oven and throws in a pork roast smothered with garlic and Italian seasonings. Soon, the aroma is infiltrating throughout the house.

"That sure smells good. Who taught you how to cook Ryan?" Greta asks.

"I used to watch my mom cook and living on your own you pick up a few things." Ryan replies with a smile.

"This guy wouldn't be bad to have around the house. He has a good job and he can cook too." Greta says as she and Cheryl both bust out laughing.

"He is my guardian angel." Cheryl says as she cuddle with Ryan on the couch.

When dinner is served, a pork roast, eight large potatoes, ten large carrots and one onion are wiped out. The girls clean off the table and wash the dishes. Greta and the kids work on a gingerbread house in the kitchen while Cheryl and Ryan relax on the couch.

"Thank you," Cheryl says to Ryan

"For what?" Ryan asks.

"For everything, the house we are living in, the food you put on the table and most of all for being here to pick me up in my hour of need." Cheryl says softly in Ryan's ear.

Cheryl kisses Ryan on the lips deeply and passionately. One kiss lead to another as Ryan embraces Cheryl with another kiss. Soon they are in a make out session on the couch. That's until Michael comes running in to the great room.

"Mommy, Mommy come and see the gingerbread house we built." Michael yells as he stands behind the couch.

"I'll be right back. Don't go anywhere." Cheryl says as she gets up.

Cheryl follows Michael into the kitchen. Ryan can hear Cheryl saying how beautiful the gingerbread house is. Ryan relaxes and puts his feet up on the ottoman and waits for Cheryl. She takes a few extra minutes and when she returns she has a handful of chocolate walnut cookies with one big glass of milk. She is careful as she sits down next to Ryan not to spill the milk.

"Where is mine?" Ryan asks.

"I share." Cheryl replies as she puts a cookie up to Ryan's mouth.

Ryan takes a bite of the soft moist cookies. He follows it down with a small sip of milk. Cheryl puts the rest of the cookie in her mouth.

"Got milk?" Ryan asks.

Cheryl smiles because her mouth is full. She hands Ryan the glass a milk but he has to pay the price with a kiss. Ryan plants a kiss on Cheryl's lips as she lets go of the glass of milk.

"Ryan and mommy sitting in a tree, K I S S I N G. First comes love, then comes marriage." Michael says from inside the kitchen doorway.

"I wouldn't go any farther than that mister." Cheryl says as she gets up off the couch and chases after Michael.

Michael hobbles into the dining room. Cheryl chases him into the dining room and when he comes through the doorway into the foyer, Ryan picks him up and carries him over to the couch. Ryan tickles Michael under his armpits and then he gives him the claw. Michael giggles and laughs out loud. Then Cheryl, Greta and Danielle jump into the mix and help Ryan tickle Michael.

"Oh God, please stop, your killing me, stop, please stop." Michael yells as he squirms and tries to get away.

After a couple of minutes of tickling Michael they finally back off. Cheryl and Danielle are laughing out loud hard and obnoxiously. Michael gets up mad and stammers off into the kitchen.

"That was good," Cheryl says while she tries to calm down.

"We had him going." Danielle says as she sits on the couch.

It is a fun filled day filled with plenty of excitement. The kids and Ryan are done with school and work until after the holidays. The excitement for the kids is building as Christmas nears. That night everyone goes to bed with a smile on their faces.

Chapter 24 – The Unexpected House Guests

On Saturday December 20th, everyone got to sleep in with the exception of Greta. She had to work until noon to get her hours in for the week. In the morning, Cheryl and Danielle go down to the church to help out with the Christmas play. Ryan and Michael bring in more firewood and go shopping for tonight's dinner. They go to Boyd's to get something special. They both wave at Greta as they walk by her at the customer service desk. The first stop is the produce section.

"What shall we get?" Ryan asks Michael.

"I don't know," Michael replies.

"How about a big tossed salad for starters." Ryan says as he points to the packaged salad.

"Oh yeah, I like salad." Michael replies.

Michael grabs the bagged salad while Ryan gets a cucumber, tomato, and an onion. Ryan also grabs a head of cauliflower and throws that in the cart.

"What are you doing with the white broccoli?" Michael asks.

"What did you call this?" Ryan replies as he does a double take back to Michael.

"White broccoli." Michael replies.

"It's a cauliflower." Ryan replies while trying to hold back his laughter.

They grab a ten pound bag of potatoes and then it's off to the meat department. Ryan walks down the counter looking for something good to cook. He looks at the steaks, chicken and pork chops. Nothing is catching his eye until he see a pork tenderloin. He pulls it out of the cooler and puts in his cart.

"What's that?" Michael asks.

"That would be heavenly goodness. It's called a pork tenderloin and I'm going to season it and grill it." Ryan replies.

Ryan and Michael finish up by grabbing a carrot cake and a loaf of bread from the bakery. Ryan grabs a cup of coffee on his way out.

"How about buying an old homeless man a cup of that coffee?" The old man asks.

"Sure, grab a cup." Ryan answers as he pays the cashier for both cups.

"Thank you," The old man replies as he drinks the cup of coffee with both hands wrapped around the foam cup.

"You're welcome." Ryan states as he pushes the cart to the checkout line.

The old man follows Ryan to the checkout. The old man hobbles as he walks. His old body is hunched over and aging. Ryan puts all the items on the conveyer.

"I need to tell you something." The old man says.

"Go ahead, I'm listening." Ryan says like he is not paying attention.

"Something bad is going to happen to Cheryl. You need to step up if she is going to live." The old man states.

"What's going to happen to her?" Ryan asks because the old man now has his attention.

"I can't tell you that, but you will let you know what you need to do when the time is near." The old man says.

"That will be twenty-three dollars and fifty-nine cents." The casher says.

Ryan turns to the cashier and hands her thirty dollars. When he turns back towards the old man he is gone. Ryan walks out beyond the cashiers lines and the old man is nowhere to be seen. Ryan shrugs off the old man comments thinking he is senile. Ryan collects his change and he and Michael head out to the car. They load the groceries into the car and head home. Ryan pulls into the driveway and rolls his window down. He asks the deputies about an update on Todd. The answer is, he is still at large. When they get into the house the first thing Ryan does is season the meat.

The afternoon flies by as Michael and Ryan watch a little TV and eat a few Christmas cookies. By three in the afternoon, Cheryl and Danielle have returned from the church. Greta gets home about an hour after that.

"I thought you only had to work until noon?" Cheryl asks Greta.

"So did I but Harriett called in sick, so I had to stay on until her replacement could get in to work." Greta replies.

Meanwhile in in the kitchen, Ryan has the cauliflower steaming, the tossed salad is put together, potatoes are boiling on the stovetop, and the Italian bread is cut and placed in a wicker serving basket.

"Honey, can you take care of what is on the stovetop. I'm going out to grill the meat." Ryan says to Cheryl.

"Sure what needs to be done?" Cheryl replies as she walks into the kitchen from the great room.

"The cauliflower needs to cook for about three more minutes. When it's done just shut it off and pull it off the burner. The potatoes are done just strain them and mash them up." Ryan says as he puts his coat on.

Ryan takes the pork tenderloin out of the fridge and heads out on the back deck. He lights the grill and lets it preheat for about five minutes. Then he puts the two pork tenderloins on the grill. Immediately they start to sizzle and cook. Ryan can smell the meat cooking which makes his mouth water. Inside Greta is upstairs changing out her work clothes while Cheryl is mashing the potatoes. Michael walks into the kitchen with a strange look on his face.

"What's wrong Michael?" Cheryl asks with a worried look on her face.

"There are two strange old people standing in the doorway." Michael says.

Cheryl quickly stops mashing the potatoes and runs towards the front door. In the doorway are two senior citizens. The female is standing behind the wheelchair where an elderly man is sitting.

"Can I help you?" Cheryl says with her hands on her hips.

"The question is can I help you. This is our house and what are you doing here?" The woman says.

Cheryl is caught off guard and doesn't know what to say. Michael instinctively runs outside to get Ryan.

The woman starts to take off her winter jacket and scarf. The man just sits in the wheelchair staring at Cheryl. Ryan comes running in with Michael hobbling behind him as he still favors his sore leg.

"Cheryl, what's going on and who is here?" Ryan says as he walks into the great room.

"Ryan, what in God's name is going on here?" The woman asks.

"Mom, dad what are you doing here?" Ryan says with a look of surprise.

Cheryl turns around and looks at Ryan with a stare that could burn a hole through him.

"There better be a good explanation for this" The woman says.

"Yes Ryan, there better be a good explanation for this." Cheryl replies.

"Let's do this calmly over a good meal and a glass of wine." Ryan says as he gives his mom and dad a hug.

Ryan goes back outside to finish cooking the meat. Cheryl helps Ryan's elderly parents into the great room. Cheryl goes back into the kitchen and finishes up the potatoes.

"Need some help?" Ryan's mother Carol asks Cheryl as she walks into the kitchen.

"No, I'm almost done here. By the way I'm Cheryl and the two children sitting out there are mine. The little boy is Michael and the girl is Danielle. Mrs. DeCicero I' am so sorry. Ryan told us the house belong to his friend's parents and they live in Florida for the winter. He told us they said we could live here for a few months until we can find a place of our own." Cheryl says with tears welling up in her eyes.

"Calm down there dear, any friend of my sons is a friend of ours. We will figure this out and no one will be left out in the cold. I just want to see my son sweat over dinner." Carol says as she comforts Cheryl.

Carol is a tall slender woman with short gray hair. She is in good shape for her age because she likes to walk a lot. Carol is a retired nurse and collects her pension and social security. She and her husband Dan have been married for forty-two years. She takes care of Dan who was stricken with ALS (Amyotrophic Lateral Sclerosis) better known as Lou Gehrig's disease. Dan is in the middle stages of the disease and he is starting to lose his ability to walk while his motor functions decrease with the disease. Dan can still talk and feed himself but he is losing his ability to be left alone. Dan is a thin man with a thick head of gray hair parted on the side. He wears wireless framed glasses and he is cleaned shaven. Dan is a retired lawyer and was a partner in a large firm specializing in criminal defense. Dan retire a few years back when he was diagnosed with ALS. Dan and Carol are well off and money is not an issue. They have always wanted Ryan to get married but he never found the right person.

"Let's eat," Ryan says as everyone takes a seat at the eight seat dining room table.

Cheryl and Ryan bring everything in and place it on the dining room table. It's a family style meal as they pass around all the dishes. Ryan opens a bottle of wine and pours it for everyone with the exception of the kids. Ryan explains everything to his parents and they are understanding. Dinner is a big hit for Dan and Carol because they love family get-together's. After dinner, Cheryl serves up the carrot cake with coffee. Dan, Greta and kids go into the great room to watch a little TV while Carol, Ryan and Cheryl remain in the dining room.

"So your ex-husband is stalking you and your kids. That's just horrible." Carol says in a distraught voice.

"The man is insane." Ryan says.

"I would say so. You have such a beautiful family Cheryl, why would he do this to you." Carol says as she takes a sip of coffee.

"Lust and money." Cheryl replies.

"So mom, please tell why you and dad are here. You two never travel up north during the winter months." Ryan asks.

"You know your dad is sick. He wants to enjoy one last Christmas with you." Carol says with a tear falling from her face.

Cheryl gets up and sits next to Carol to help console her.

"That's no problem mom, I love when you two are here with me. We will have a good old fashioned family Christmas." Ryan says as he kisses his mom on the forehead.

"Thank you so much Ryan." Carol replies as she wipes the tears from her eyes with a napkin.

The sleeping arrangements are made. One of the couches pulls out into a sleeper and that is where Carol and Dan will sleep. This way Dan doesn't have to be carried to the bedroom located on the second floor.

By eleven o'clock everyone is in bed with the exception of Cheryl. She is still cleaning up the dishes from dinner and dessert. Cheryl closes the door to the dishwasher when Carol walks into the kitchen carrying a small booklet. Carol is dressed in her nightgown that is covered by a heavy blue terrycloth robe.

"Cheryl, come over here and take a seat." Carol says as she sits at the breakfast island.

Cheryl walks over with hot kettle of water.

"Carol, would you like a cup of tea?" Cheryl asks.

"Oh yes that sounds good." Carol replies as Cheryl pour the water into a cup.

Cheryl grabs the milk and sugar holder as she sets them on the island. They both fix their tea the way they like it. Carol sets the booklet on the table and Cheryl recognizes it.

"That's my eighth grade year book." Cheryl says with a surprise.

"Close my dear, this is Ryan's eighth grade year book." Carol says with a snicker.

"What is so special about his year book?" Cheryl asks.

Carol opens up the yearbook to Ryan's picture. There is a nerdy boy with glasses, braces, and a face full of zits.

"Look at this poor boy. Do you know how many times he came home from school dejected about this young lady in his class? He always had the same response, she will never take a second look at me" Carol says.

Cheryl gets the idea of where this conversation is going and she just listens. Carol turns the page in the old year book. She turns to the page where Cheryl's picture is located. Cheryl looks hard at the picture and sees something written below her picture. It reads *"Someday I hope you see me for the man I will be. I see you look over at me in class and then I realize you're looking right through me like I am not even there. Someday you will see me for who I really am and that's the day you will become my girlfriend."*

"Oh my god, Ryan wrote that twenty years ago?" Cheryl says with tears in her eyes.

"He had a crush on you like there was no tomorrow. He would come home from school and talk about you like you were his best friend." Carol replies.

"I didn't know." Cheryl says as she wipes a tear from her eye.

"You wouldn't have known. He was so shy when he was a kid I would have to push him to go to school functions." Carol replies as the two women hug each other.

"Carol, he has done so much for me and the kids. I don't know how to repay him." Cheryl replies with tears running out of both eyes.

"I see a gleam in his eyes when he looks at you. I have never seen that look of happiness before." Carol replies.

"You really think he has that look in his eyes?" Cheryl asks.

"Take a long hard look at him the next time he is looking at you. Mark my words you will see it." Carol says.

They finish their tea and turn off the lights in the kitchen. Upon exiting the kitchen Carol whispers in Cheryl ear.

"This is our little secret." Carol whispers in Cheryl's ear followed by a little hug.

Chapter 25 – Sunday Mass

On Sunday morning everyone is up early and goes to mass. After mass the group of seven prepare to go out for brunch when they run into Gracie. She walks past Cheryl and her grandkids with her head down. She is so ashamed of how she acted and how her son treated his own wife and children. Cheryl being the good person she is, goes out of her way to say hello.

"Hi Gracie, how are you today?" Cheryl asks.

"I'm ok and I'm just afraid of what Todd is capable off." Gracie replies with her head down avoiding eye contact.

"Hey what are you doing after mass?" Cheryl asks.

"I'm going home to be alone." Gracie respond dejectedly.

"Why don't you join us for brunch and then we are coming back to the parish for the Christmas play." Cheryl asks.

"I don't want to impose." Gracie says as she walks away.

"You're not imposing, come on you are welcome to join us." Ryan says.

Gracie smiles and accepts the invitation. They go out and have brunch at the Springside. Everyone is smiling, laughing and enjoying each other's company. Gracie even gets into the conversation. During brunch Gracie has a heart to heart with Danielle. When they finish up their dessert and coffee, they prepare to go to the play. Gracie gets up and thanks Cheryl and Ryan for inviting her to enjoy the day with them.

"Gracie, what are you doing for Christmas Eve and Christmas Day?" Ryan asks.

"Probably staying home, why?" Gracie replies.

"Because we are having dinner both days and we would like you there to celebrate with us." Cheryl says.

"You better make enough food because your sister is coming in for Christmas too." Carol replies.

"You know me mom, I like to cook for an army. Cheryl and I will make out the menu tonight." Ryan replies.

"The more the merrier." Danielle says as she butts in.

After brunch, Ryan pays the entire tab as they head back to the parish to see the play. At the church everyone sits together in one row with Dan at the end sitting in his wheelchair. The play is about an hour and fifteen minutes long. The play finishes and everyone heads towards the door. As they are leaving the church it begins to snow heavily. The snow piles up quickly at the rate of one to two inches per hour.

"What shall we have for dinner?" Cheryl asks.

"How about some pasta." Carol replies.

"I don't have any sauce." Cheryl says.

"Then we will make some." Ryan says.

Ryan and Cheryl run to the store and buy what they need to make sauce plus hamburger and sausage. The entire afternoon Cheryl, Ryan, and Carol work together in the kitchen making the sauce. Ryan mixes the meatballs while Cheryl fries up the sausage. Carol is busy putting the sauce together.

"Boy that smells good." Gracie says as she walks into the kitchen.

"Wait until it's done." Ryan says with a grin.

By six o'clock everyone is at the table eating. A tossed salad, angel hair pasta, meatballs, sausage and crusty Italian bread. A traditional Italian Sunday dinner that includes wine. The conversation is friendly and full of laughter. Then there is a knock on the door as it goes silent in the dining room. They can hear adults and children voices talking on the porch. Ryan gets up to answer the door.

"I think I know who it is?" Carol says.

"Jennifer, Randy and the kids." Ryan replies.

Ryan opens the door and outside is his kid sister Jennifer and her family. Jennifer stands about five feet seven inches tall with long dark hair. She has gained a little weight but still looks good. She is twenty-nine years old with beautiful facial features and big brown eyes. Jennifer has perfect teeth and a beautiful smile. She is a stay at home mom with two young children. Stevie is her six year old son. He has sandy brown hair with brown eyes like his mother. Stevie is a mischievous kid that gets into everything. Maria is a darling little three year old. She has long dark hair with blue eyes that she gets from her father. Randy on the other hand is tall and heavy set. He has gained a lot of weight and been diagnosed with type one diabetes. He is balding but sports a full beard with blue eyes. Randy works as a radio sports announcer for the Tampa Bay Rays.

"Jennifer, you look absolutely stunning." Ryan says as hugs his sister.

"Ryan, how are you big brother." Jennifer says.

"I'm good and I'm so glad you're here with us." Ryan says.

The four family members come into the house. All the introductions are done as they take a seat at the table. Carol and Cheryl get out four plates and serve them dinner. The dining room starts to get loud with talking and children making noise. Soon enough Dan, Randy and Ryan go out into the living room to watch some football. The girls are talking and laughing like they are in a soap opera. When the football game ends Ryan gets an idea.

"Who would like to go sledding?" Ryan asks.

"I do, I do." Michael says.

"Sounds like fun to me." Danielle replies.

"Jennifer how about you, Randy and the kids." Ryan was with enthusiasm.

"I don't know," Jennifer says with skepticism.

"Come on it would be like old times." Ryan replies.

"Oh alright, let me get the kids all bundled up." Jennifer says.

"Randy, are you coming?" Ryan asks.

"I'm going to have to pass Ryan. I'll stay here and watch the Sunday Night football game with your father." Randy replies while taking a sip of beer.

"Are you coming honey." Ryan says to Cheryl.

"No, I have to clean up this mess." Cheryl replies as she starts to gather up the dinner plates.

"Nonsense honey, we got this." Carol says as she takes the plates out of Cheryl's hands.

"Go and have a little fun." Greta says.

"Are you sure?" Cheryl asks.

"Yes, go and have a good time." Gracie says as she picks the glasses up off the table.

They all bundle up and go out into the fresh new snow. Ryan pulls the toboggan, two sleds and two saucers that are stored in the garage. Behind the house there is a two hundred foot hill that is perfect for sledding. When they get to the top the kids are looking down with excitement.

"Okay the first thing we have to do is make a trail." Ryan says.

"How do we do that?" Michael asks.

"Well we all get on the toboggan and flatten the track. Then we are home free to sled." Ryan says with a smile.

So Ryan gets on the front. Cheryl sits behind him. Then Danielle, Michael, Stevie, Maria, and finally Jennifer. They use their hands to get the toboggan moving. Slowly the toboggan goes down the hill. Faster and faster they go. The light snow is whipping up and over the sled into everyone's face. Everyone is laughing with the exception of little Maria, she is screaming and frightened. As the night goes along one by one each person heads back to the house because they are cold. First to go are Jennifer and Maria. Then Danielle and both Michael and Stevie. This leaves Cheryl and Ryan on top of the hill together.

"Maybe we should be getting back too?" Cheryl asks.

"One more time. Just you and I." Ryan says as he lays on his stomach on the toboggan.

Cheryl looks at Ryan like he is nuts.

"Come on climb on my back." Ryan says.

Cheryl is a little reluctant but does as he says. She lays on top of his back with her arms wrapped around his side. Ryan has the ropes in his hands as he pulls his feet back onto the toboggan. Slowly the sled releases and starts its trek down the hill. The toboggan picks up speed and flies down the now icy trail. They reach speeds of thirty-five to forty miles per hour. The toboggan flies down the hill and into the snow where the trail ends. Snow flies everywhere and covers both Ryan and Cheryl. When the toboggan comes to a stop they both look like snowmen. They are totally covered with snow. Both of them are laughing out loud as they get off the toboggan. Cheryl has snow all over face, down her neck and inside her boots. Ryan's face is cover with snow, and he lost his left glove on the way down.

"That was great," Ryan says as he stands up.

"Yes it was." Cheryl says as she brushes the snow off herself.

They both clean the snow off each other. They walk up the hill together holding hands. Ryan is pulling the toboggan with his left hand while they look for his lost glove. They get halfway up the hill when Cheryl sees the glove.

"There it is." Cheryl says as she point towards the glove sticking straight up out of the snow.

Ryan bends down to pick up the glove when Cheryl shoves him for fun. Ryan loses his balance and falls backwards onto the toboggan. He reaches and grabs Cheryl and as he pulls her down on the toboggan also. Ryan lands on his back and Cheryl is facing him. The toboggan begins to go down the hill again.

"Here we go again." Cheryl says while laughing.

The toboggan goes down the hill out of control. Snow is fling up and all over them again. Ryan puts his arms around Cheryl as they fly into the fluffy snow at the bottom of the hill. Both of them are laughing out of control. When the toboggan comes to a stop they are in hysterics. Ryan puts both hands up and clutches Cheryl's cheeks.

"You are so beautiful." Ryan says as he guides their lips together.

Cheryl and Ryan lay on top of the toboggan as a harmless kiss turns into a passionate kiss. They lay totally snow covered with arms wrapped around each other enthralled in a passionate kiss that lasts well over a minute.

"We better get back." Cheryl says as she breaks the kiss.

"Not until you kiss me again." Ryan replies as he gazes into her eyes.

Cheryl is hypnotized with Ryan as she bends down and kisses him deeply again. This time the kiss lasts over two minutes. When they finally break and come up for air Ryan can see Cheryl wants him to kiss her again. Ryan pulls Cheryl face close to him and they kiss again. When they finish with that kiss Cheryl gets off the sled and stands up. Ryan follows as they brush the snow off again.

"How about some hot chocolate?" Cheryl asks Ryan as they walk up the hill again.

"You read my mind." Ryan says as he reaches to hold Cheryl's hand again.

They walk back to the house in the cold and snowy night. Hand in hand they walk into the garage first. Ryan hangs the toboggan up on the wall. He grabs the other sleds that everyone left on the floor and hangs them on the wall as well. Cheryl brushes off all the loose snow as she takes her coat and boots off. Ryan follows suit and before they walk into the house they capture one more kiss together. They walk into the house and everyone is in the great room watching the football game. They are all rooting and yelling at the TV.

"Go see what all the fuss is. I'll get our hot chocolate." Cheryl says.

Ryan walks into the great room and time is expiring in the game. The Minnesota Vikings are on the Green Bay Packers five yard line with five seconds left in the game and down by five points. Everyone is still there with the exception of Gracie who went home.

"You should have seen this game Ryan. The Vikings were down twenty-six points going into the fourth quarter and here they are on the brink of stealing this game." Dan says from his wheelchair.

It all quiet in the house as the final play from scrimmage is snapped.

"The ball is snapped to Matt Cassel and he fakes the handoff to Adrian Peterson. Peterson is hit at the line of scrimmage. Cassel tucks the ball under his arm and is running to his left. All the receivers in front of him are covered. It looks like Clay Matthews is closing in on Cassel. He has nowhere to run. Everyone is covered in the end zone, wait, Cassel turns and starts to run to his right. There is Adrian Peterson all alone in the corner of the end zone. Cassel throws the ball. There is no one covering him. The ball is caught and it's a touchdown. The Minnesota Vikings have just come back from twenty-six down to beat the Packers on the final play of the game. Not only did they just steal this game from the Packers but they have won the division." The announcer yells with emotion.

"Wow, Ryan you missed one hell of a game." Randy says.

Cheryl brings Ryan his hot chocolate. Ryan takes a sip while everyone prepares for bed. Everyone is sleeping in the same place from the night before with the exception Stevie will sleep up in Michael's room. Jennifer, Randy and Maria are sleeping on the blow up bed covered with a feather bed. That bed is set up in the great room in between the pull out bed that Carol and Dan are sleeping on and the couch that Ryan is sleeping on.

"Wow, we have a full house." Cheryl says to Ryan in the kitchen.

"You got that right." Ryan replies.

They work together to get the dishwasher emptied and reloaded. All the dinner dishes have been put away and the dessert and snack dishes are loaded in the dishwasher. Cheryl closes up the dishwasher as Ryan comes up behind her and puts his arms around her waist. He kisses her softly on the back of her neck. Cheryl puts her head back enjoying the attention.

"If you keep that up you're going to have to take me to bed. I don't think we have anywhere to do that. Every room in this house is occupied." Cheryl whispers in Ryan ear.

"The stairway is empty." Ryan replies.

"No, were not going to make love for the first time on the stairway. I want it to be special." Cheryl says as she turns around and kisses Ryan on the lips.

"That would be special." Ryan says trying to coax Cheryl into saying yes.

Cheryl slaps him on the shoulder.

"No, not tonight with everyone here." Cheryl says as she hugs Ryan tightly.

Cheryl kisses Ryan one more time before she heads towards the stairway to go upstairs. She blows him a kiss as she walks through the door into the great room.

"Goodnight," Cheryl says as she walks through the great room and heads up the stairs.

Ryan leans against the kitchen counter and watches Cheryl as she walks away. He grabs a big glass and fills it with ice cold water. He drinks down the entire glass of water before retiring for the night.

Chapter 26 – Monday December 22nd

On Monday morning Greta and Cheryl are the only two that have to get up and go to work. They are up bright and early as they shower one after the other. Ryan gets up when he hears the water running upstairs. He goes into the kitchen and starts to make a pot of coffee. The coffee is brewing and Carol comes into the kitchen with her robe covering up her night gown.

"Good morning Ryan," Carol says.

"Morning mom, how did you sleep?" Ryan asks.

"Alright I guess," Carol replies.

"Why, what kept you up?" Ryan asks.

"The snoring battle between you and Randy." Carol says with a smile.

Ryan and Carol fix their coffee and drink it at the island in the kitchen. This way the noise will not carry through the house and wake everyone else up. Within a couple of minutes both Cheryl and Greta come down the stairs and into the kitchen. They both pour some coffee into a travel mug and head towards the door.

"Hey, when I get home tonight we need to figure out the holiday meals. I'm thinking some kind of meat and fixings for Christmas Eve and lasagna for Christmas day. Let me know what you think about that." Cheryl says as she gives Ryan a kiss on the lips.

Ryan nods his head yes as he agrees on the menu. Both women head out the door to go to work at Boyd's. With only three days until Christmas the store is going to be hectic. Both women expect that because they have been there on previous Christmas's and worked through it. As the car starts and pulls away, Ryan gets up from the table to fill his cup again.

"You know those kids have never had a good Christmas before. Have you bought them anything yet?" Carol asks Ryan.

"All taken care of mom. They are going to be ecstatic when they unwrap the gifts I bought for them." Ryan states.

"How about Cheryl?" Carol asks.

"Taken care of mom, just like I have taken care of you, dad and Jennifer and her family." Ryan says with a smile.

"You are so generous with your money and time, how has it taken this long to find someone?" Carol asks.

"I just had to find the right person." Ryan answers.

"Well I'm just letting you know you have my approval on this one. Cheryl is a beautiful person with a great personality and she is smart too." Carol says as she sips her coffee.

"Thanks mom, your approval means a lot me." Ryan says with a chuckle.

As the day goes by, Ryan runs some errands and buys a few more gifts for Cheryl and the rest of the family. He even stops in at the store to have lunch with Cheryl. They grab a sub with a salad and split it. They talk about Christmas Eve and Christmas Day dinner. It's agreed that prime rib will be served on Christmas Eve and lasagna with all the fixings will be served on Christmas Day. Then Ryan's cell phone rings. He walks outside to hear the caller because the noise level is too high inside the store. Cheryl remains at the table picking at the salad when all of a sudden the old man sits down at the table with her.

"Cheryl, I am here to help you. Your life is in danger. Please do as I say and stay home. All I can tell you is if you don't listen to me you are not going to see Christmas Day." The old man says.

This startles Cheryl as she gets up from the table and backs away. Cheryl walks right into the table behind her as she trips and falls to the ground. The person sitting at that table helps her back to her feet.

"Are you alright miss?" The patron at the table asks.

"That man at my table, he, he." Cheryl stutters to the patron.

To Cheryl surprise, there is no one sitting at her table. She looks around and the old man is nowhere to be seen. Everyone sitting in the deli area is looking at Cheryl like she is on drugs. Then Ryan returns and sees Cheryl with a frightened look on her face. Ryan runs to her side and sits her back down. Cheryl explains to Ryan what the man said to her. Ryan takes it in and tries to put it all together. Ryan tells Cheryl of his conversation that he had with the old man a couple days ago. Both of them are spooked and can't understand who he is and what he wants.

"Cheryl, I am here and I'm not going to let anything happen to you." Ryan says as he hugs her tight.

"I'm really scared Ryan, I think this man is stalking me." Cheryl says in Ryan's arms.

"Just calm down honey. We have each other and he won't hurt you in the store. There are too many people here. He won't come to the house because we have a full house and two deputies outside." Ryan says as he strokes the back of her head.

Ryan remains at the store for the rest of the day. He makes sure he picks up everything needed for the Christmas Eve and Christmas Day dinners. Ryan even picks up five pounds of shrimp for both days. At the end of Cheryl's shift the three of them walk out to the car together. They drive to house with both cars one in front of the other.

Meanwhile, Todd is still spying on Cheryl on a daily basis. He watches her at work and he even has gotten close to the house at night to watch. Little did Todd know he could have had Cheryl on Sunday night while they were sledding but he was in the abandoned building puking his guts out. Somewhere over the past twenty four hours Todd contracted the flu. There he lays on the dirty mattress in a cold and damp building throwing up in a bucket. He has the chills and bundles up with a dirty old blanket and a canvas tarp. Todd tries some over the counter drugs but they do little or nothing for him. He cannot sleep because the cold weather is eating right through his layers and the blankets.

"What the hell am I thinking staying here? I'm broke with no car or means of getting out of this hell hole. I could turn myself in and get a warm bed and three squares a day. The hell with that if I'm going to spend the rest of my life behind bars, my ex-wife is going to pay dearly." Todd says as he rolls onto his back.

While Todd is laying there in the darkness he hears something downstairs on the concrete floor. Slowly he rolls off the mattress. He tries not to make any noises as he gets to his feet. The wooden floor below his feet is old and rotten. One foot in front of the other Todd walks towards the office window overlooking the floor below. When he reaches the window there are flashlights shining all over the floor below. Todd can hear the police officer scurrying around searching for him or someone else. Todd is always thinking ahead as he walks with urgency but tries to be as quiet as he can. He figures he has two minutes maybe three to make his escape or the police will be all over him. Todd walks towards the outer wall that has one window overlooking the river. The only problem is the window is blocked with an old air conditioner. Todd first tries to pull the air conditioner inside but he can't because it's wedged in from the outside.

"Hey detective, there is a staircase here." A police officer says in a whisper but Todd can hear him.

Todd tries one last time to pull the air conditioner inside but it doesn't budge. Todd struggles with his strength due to his illness. Todd can hear the wooden stairs creaking as the police officers are climbing up the stairs. Todd can feel the adrenaline flowing through his veins and with one monstrous push against the air conditioner, it dislodges. Then he pushes the unit out the window. It makes a loud crashing sound against the side of the building just before it splashes into the running water below.

"What was that?" a police officer yells

"He is upstairs in the office." The detective tells to his men.

Todd quickly climbs on the window ledge. He looks down and can see the water rushing below him. He looks around for other options but there is nowhere else to go. Todd assess how many feet the jump will be before he hits the water. Then the police kick the door in and Todd jumps into the freezing cold water below. The twenty foot drop is nothing compared to the ice cold rushing water below. Todd hits the water below and is swept away in the current. The water drags him quickly and swiftly downstream. Todd tries to swim to the banks of the river but he cannot get there because the current is dragging him towards the center. Todd can feel the ice cold water biting into his flesh. Even though he is already ill, this could finish him off. Todd continues to swim and he can feel his strength fading away. Todd knows hypothermia only takes minutes and his fingers and toes are already starting to become numb. Within three or four minutes the current has carried him one third of mile away from the building. Finally, the current slows down and into a pool of slow moving water. Todd seizes the moment and swims to the opposite side of the river. When he gets out of the freezing cold water, the wind and cold temperatures only makes it feel colder. Todd quickly starts to climb up the thirty foot embankment. When he is about half way up he can hear the police sirens driving on the opposite side of the river. Todd knows they have to cross the bridge to get where he is and that is three miles downriver. This should give him ample time to get out of the area and find a place to hide.

"I need to get out of these wet clothes and find a place to warm up." Todd says as he reaches the top of the embankment.

Todd comes up in the backyard of a house. He runs towards the front of the house. He crosses the road and runs up a side street. Todd can hear the sirens as the police converge on the location where he climbed up the embankment. Todd knows his footprints can be seen in the fresh fallen snow in the yard of the house. When Todd crosses the street his footprint are gone because the roads have been plowed down to the pavement. Todd uses his head as he runs on the road away from the scene. He knows it's going to take a few minutes to find his tracks and by then he should be off the road. As Todd fades over the top of the hill he can see the flashing blue and red lights on top of the police cars. Todd looks at his watch and he times three minutes because that is when the police cars will be driving around the area looking for him or another set of prints. Todd runs hard until he gets outside the city limits. Then he can see the red and blue lights of the police car glowing over the horizon. Todd knows the police car is driving up the same road he is running on. He knows he has to get off the road now but he doesn't want to make a trail in the snow.

"Oh my god yes." Todd says as he see a completely shoveled driveway.

This person shoveled the driveway right down to the pavement. Todd dashes towards the driveway and runs down it. He sees a high snow bank that he dives over it just as the police car comes into view. Todd stays down behind the snowbank as the police car slowly creeps up on his position. Todd is freezing cold as he remains still and well hidden. Todd can hear the car tires on the pavement and then he hears the squealing brakes as the police car comes to a stop. Todd remains still but he is breathing heavily as he remains calm. Then the spot light on the police car turns on. The light shines towards Todd but into the backyard. Todd can see the light dancing across the snow as it shimmers.

"Unit 12 there is a report of someone moving around in a backyard off of 1st Ave." A female voice says over the radio.

"Dispatch, we are responding." One of the officers in the car replies.

The police car turns around in the same driveway that Todd is hiding in. Todd remains still as he can hear the car back out of the driveway. Todd waits until the car drives off. Then he pops his head up and looks up and down the road. He can see the police cars rear lights as they glow off in the distance. Todd gets to his feet and runs into the backyard and off into the darkness. Todd runs for two miles into the farm lands of central New York. During his run Todd finds an old coat in a parked pickup truck. Then he steals some clothes off a clothes line. Todd quickly changes into the dry clothes but he is still chilled to the bone.

"Got to find someplace to warm up." Todd says as he runs through the fields.

Then he comes across an old hay building. The building has just a roof with six wooden poles on a concrete slab. The building is filled with hay but it is open on all four sides. Todd quickly creates a shelter with the hay. He gathers some fire wood from an old dead elm tree. He piles some of wood and starts a fire. He sets the remaining wood aside for later on. Todd breaks a bale of hay and spreads it across the concrete floor. The remaining hay he sets on top of him to help keep him warm. Todd slowly fights off the cold night as the fire burns warm. Todd falls asleep quickly from being ill and cold. The hay helps insulates Todd and warms his body quickly.

Chapter 27 – The Preparation for Christmas

On Tuesday December 23rd the anticipation for Christmas is driving the children crazy. They are running around the house screaming and yelling like they are on a sugar high. The adults have a hard time keeping them away from the Christmas tree and looking at their gifts. Ryan works diligently preparing the food for the holiday. He seasons the prime rib, prepares the shrimp and puts together two platters of lasagna. Greta and Cheryl both have to work a half day. When they return to the house Cheryl sees what Ryan is doing.

"Hey honey, what are you doing?" Cheryl asks as she gives Ryan a kiss.

"Just getting a head start for tomorrow's dinner and Christmas dinner." Ryan replies.

"Wow that prime rib looks good." Cheryl replies.

"Wait until you taste it." Ryan says.

Cheryl goes upstairs and changes out of her work clothes. She comes back downstairs and helps Ryan work on the preparing the food. Carol and Greta help out in the kitchen while Randy and Dan sit in the great room and watch TV. The kids go outside and play in the snow as Christmas is coming quickly. Then there is a knock on the door. Ryan and Cheryl answer the door together. Standing outside is one of the deputies from the car.

"Yes deputy, what can we do for you?" Ryan asks.

"Please tell me you apprehended him?" Cheryl pleads.

"I just wanted to inform you that we almost apprehended Todd yesterday in an abandoned shop by the outlet. He escaped by jumping into the river and eluding us while we tried to apprehend him. The reason why I'm here is we found something he was planning. It looks like something to do with St Anthony's Church on the 24th." The deputy says.

"We were planning on going to midnight mass." Cheryl replies.

"If Todd has not been apprehended by then, I would advise against going to mass." The deputy says as he turns around and heads back to his car.

"Thank you," Ryan says as the deputy walks away.

Ryan closes the door and Cheryl runs to the bathroom. Ryan runs behind her but she closes the door before he can catch up to her. Cheryl locks the door and sits on the toilet crying. Ryan can hear her crying through the door.

"What's wrong Cheryl?" Ryan's asks as he lightly knocks on the door.

"How does that bastard continue to evade the law? That man has ruined my life and it just won't stop. I have never missed midnight mass." Cheryl says as she cries.

"Cheryl if you want to go to midnight mass, then we are going no matter what." Ryan replies.

Cheryl opens the door and engulfs herself into Ryan's arms.

"We can't let him hold us hostage." Ryan says as he tries to reinsure her confidence.

Cheryl and Ryan head back into the kitchen and finish up with the prep work. They put everything in the refrigerator which looks like a stuffed pig.

"You can't put anything else inside this refrigerator. Wow, that's a lot of food." Carol says as they close the door.

"What's for dinner tonight?" Cheryl asks.

"Oh shit, I didn't think about that." Ryan replies.

"Come on were all going out to dinner. It's getting a little claustrophobic in here." Carol says.

They all get dressed up in casual clothes and head out to dinner. They only place that can accommodate a party that size is Applebee's. This gives everyone a chance to get out of the house for a little bit. The table is loud with everyone talking over each other. Danielle sits with her mom and they talk about buying Ryan something for Christmas. Michael and Stevie make more noise than the entire group. Ryan gets a chance to sit with his dad and talk one on one with each other. Greta, Carol and Jennifer talk in general about Ryan and Cheryl and how they are a perfect match for each other. At the end of the day Dan and Carol pick up the tab for dinner and dessert. They head back to the house where they light up a fire and turn on all the Christmas lights.

"Come on its family time. Let's watch a movie together." Ryan says as he tries to get everyone together.

"What is this one?" Carol says as she picks a DVD out of Ryan's collection.

"It's the Polar Express. We just watched it a week or so ago." Ryan replies.

"What's it about?" Carol ask

"It's about a boy that doesn't believe in Christmas anymore and the Polar Express takes him on a journey to the North Pole on Christmas Eve." Ryan replies.

"Sounds interesting to me. Dan, do you want to watch it?" Carol asks.

"Put it in, if it quiets the kids down that will only make things tolerable." Dan replies.

They put the Polar Express into the DVD player. Ryan turns on the surround sound and then he turns off all the lights in the house with the exception of the Christmas decorations. Everyone grabs a seat with the exception of Cheryl and Ryan. They go into the kitchen and make some microwave popcorn. They pour all four bags into three large bowls and bring them into the great room. Everyone is totally enthralled into the animated movie. Cheryl hands a bowl of popcorn to the left couch and one to the right couch.

"There is nowhere to sit." Cheryl says.

"Right there on floor in-between Michael and Stevie." Ryan replies.

Everyone is watching the movie with the exception of Maria. She is sound asleep on her mother's lap.

Meanwhile out in the country, Todd is feeding his small fire and staying warm under the hay. He isn't going hungry because he stole some eggs and potatoes from the farmer down the road. He sits under the shelter figuring out his evil plot to get even with Cheryl. It's now a vendetta because Todd is blaming her for everything that went wrong with his life. Todd has always been the type of person that never takes responsibility for his own actions. Todd knows Cheryl will be at midnight mass on Christmas Eve. He knows this will be his last opportunity to get even with her. Todd no longer wants to kidnap the kids and run away. He just wants to ruin Cheryl's life.

"I'm going to take care of that bitch once and for all." Todd say as he boils a couple of eggs in a coffee can over the open fire.

Todd has two potatoes baking in the coals of the fire and two eggs boiling in the coffee can. He knows this may be all he is going to eat because the farmer is going to get suspicious if the food continues to disappear. Todd knows his mother is pissed off at him. He knows she won't give him any money and besides her house is being watched.

The evening goes by quickly as Todd finishes eating his last potato. The eggs have been peeled and eaten also. Todd gets comfortable while he spends his second night in the cold. He adds a couple more pieces of wood to the fire as he covers himself with hay. Todd has a full belly and now it's time to get some rest and get ready for his big day. Within a few minutes, Todd is fast asleep and snoring like chainsaw. By ten in the evening Todd is in rem sleep and totally tuned out to the world around him.

"Who the hell are you and what are you doing on my property?" The old farmer yells as he grabs Todd by his coat lapels.

"What, who are you?" Todd says in a sleepy voice.

"I'm the man that owns this here property. I can see you were in my barn stealing my food. One thing I can't stand is a thief." The farmer states as he pulls Todd to his feet.

"Get your hands off me old man." Todd says in a loud firm voice as he starts to regain his bearings.

"What did you say to me?' The old farmer yells as he rears back with his right hand.

Todd can see the old farmer is pissed off and he is going to assault him. Todd being proactive blocks the old man's punch and throws him to the ground. Todd brushes the hay off himself as the old farmer struggles to get to his feet.

"If I were you old man I would go back to my house before you get hurt." Todd says with determination.

"Really," The old farmer says as he gets to his feet.

Todd looks down at himself and doesn't see the old farmer move into position. When Todd looks up the old farmer blasts him in the nose. The blow sends Todd backwards into the hay stacks. Todd falls backwards onto his back when he trips over the hay stacks. Todd slowly gets up and he can feel a wetness on his face. He puts his hand under his nose to feel the wetness. Then he puts his hand out to see the red blood dripping from his broken nose. The old farmer is busy kicking snow on the open fire. Todd picks up a dead branch from the wood pile. He doesn't say a word while he creeps up behind the old farmer. When old farmer hears a twig snaps under Todd's feet, he turns towards Todd. Todd swings the branch with all his might like a baseball bat. He hits the old farmer square in the head. The old farmer falls backwards into the snow. The old farmer reaches for his head while Todd walks over the top of him.

"You should have minded your own business." Todd says as he lifts the branch over the top of his head with both hands.

"Please don't," The old farmer says as he pleads for his life.

Todd swings down on the old farmers head. The five inch circumference branch crushes the farmer's skull, killing him instantly. Todd feels no remorse and turns back towards his little camp. He finishes putting out the fire and gathers his belongings. He walks over to the farmer and checks his pockets. He takes out his wallet and steals the thirty-five dollars. Then Todd reaches into the farmer's jacket pocket and takes out a set of keys.

"You should have minded your own business and you would still be alive." Todd says as he throws the branch on the farmer's chest.

Todd walks towards the farm and leaves the farmer's body in the snow. When he reaches the farm house he can see a light on inside. He ignores the light and walks toward the pickup truck. He unlocks the door to the truck and starts it up. Todd puts the pickup into gear and starts to pull out. He looks at the windows of the house and sees an old woman looking out at him. Todd knows there is enough brightness from the snow and she will notice her husband is not driving. Todd being the ass he is, waves to the farmer's wife as he drives away. Todd knows he has to ditch the truck as soon as he gets into the city. He knows the farmer's wife is calling police and they will be looking for the pickup truck. He gets onto the highway and he puts the pedal to the metal and drives towards the city. When he gets into town he uses all the side roads to get to his destination.

"Nice truck, I'm going to have to hide you for later." Todd says as he parks the brand new truck by railroad tracks hidden behind an old warehouse.

Todd takes the keys and puts them in his coat pocket. The railroad yard is about two blocks away from St Anthony's Church. Todd walks towards the church with a hood over his head and hands in his pockets. It's dark with light snow showers that helps keep him hidden. When Todd reaches the church he finds an open door. He goes inside and finds a place to hide up in the choir on the second floor. The second floor is located at the back of the church and overhangs over the pews. There he finds warmth and a place to sleep for the night.

By midnight everyone in the house is sound asleep. The children are restless with the anticipation and excitement for all the Christmas festivities and gifts.

Chapter 28 – Christmas Eve

On Christmas Eve morning everyone is up early to prepare for the holiday. Greta and Cheryl both have to work until five in the afternoon because that is when the store closes for Christmas. They both leave the house at seven am to put in a ten hour day.

"This is going to be the day from hell." Cheryl says to Greta in the car driving to work.

"Just think when we get out of here tonight its Christmas Eve and tomorrow is Christmas Day. No work, just family and fun. We can just enjoy ourselves" Greta replies with a smile.

"I am looking forward to that." Cheryl replies.

"You know what I'm looking forward to" Greta says.

"What's that Greta?" Cheryl replies.

"Being able go home and sleep in my own bed." Greta says.

As they drive to work the news comes on the radio. The reporter says that a farmer has been murdered and the suspect is believed to be Todd LaRussa. The reporter went on the say that it's also believed that he is in hiding somewhere in the city. Both Greta and Cheryl look at each other with a look of concern.

"This is never going to end." Cheryl says.

"Just relax Cheryl, he isn't going to come into a crowded store to seek you out. He is definitely not going to come out to the house." Greta says with a reassuring voice.

When they get to work they both get out of the car and go inside together. Cheryl looks around the parking lot for Todd. She is nervous and it shows. When she reaches the door to go inside she is bumped into by someone. Cheryl lets out a slight scream as it startles her.

The day moves along quite rapidly with the volume of customers. Cheryl soon forgets about Todd and does her job. By four thirty the store is starting to clear out. Everyone is in hurry to get home and start their Christmas festivities. Cheryl walks over to the front door and looks out at the weather. The skies are gray and snow is falling. The forecast says a snow storm is expected in the evening hours. They are expecting ten inches to a foot by Christmas morning.

"He is out there and looking for you." The old man says startling Cheryl at the outer door.

"Who are you and what do you want?" Cheryl says as she starts to back away.

"You will find out soon enough who I am." The old man answers.

"You are scaring me." Cheryl says as she backs up.

"Don't be afraid of me. I am here for you. Please be aware of your surroundings I can only do so much" The old man states.

"Cheryl, who are you talking too?" Greta asks from behind the customer service desk.

"The old man." Cheryl replies.

Greta bends over the counter and doesn't see anyone. When Cheryl turns back towards the door the old man is gone. Cheryl doesn't understand who he is and how he mysteriously can appear and disappear. Cheryl walks back to the counter where she and Greta begin to lock everything up. By five fifteen the store is closed and they are leaving to go home. Greta makes a stop at her apartment to pick up some nice clothes to wear for Christmas. When they get home the smell of prime rib is rushing throughout the interior rooms of the house. The fire in the fireplace is burning bright with a slight aroma of hickory. The smell of the prime rib and hickory are mixing and they are intoxicating together.

"How long until dinner?" Cheryl asks.

"We're almost done with everything with the exception of the prime rib. The meat still has twenty minutes to cook." Ryan says as he gives Cheryl a kiss.

Everyone is already dressed up for Christmas Eve dinner. The girls and women are in dresses and the men are wearing button up shirts with khaki's.

"Okay I'm going upstairs to get dressed. I'll be down in a couple of minutes." Cheryl says.

Both Cheryl and Greta go up the stairs and into the master bedroom to change and redo their hair. Cheryl picks out a beautiful green dress that comes down to her knees. Greta has a black skirt with a white blouse. When they finish up dressing they help each other with their hair and makeup.

"Come on you look fantastic." Greta tells Cheryl

Cheryl and Greta come down the stairs and Ryan can do nothing but stare at Cheryl. She looks stunning with her hair flowing over her shoulders and dressed so elegantly.

"Wow, you look absolutely beautiful." Ryan says.

"You don't look half bad yourself." Cheryl says as they hug at the bottom of the stairs.

Cheryl and Ryan go into the kitchen where Cheryl gets herself a glass of eggnog. She takes one sip and shakes her head.

"Whoa, what's in here?" Cheryl asks.

"That would be vanilla ice cream and some whiskey." Ryan replies.

"Wow, that's got a kick to it, but it tastes good!" Cheryl says as she takes another sip.

Gracie arrives and everyone is talking and having a good time. Soon everyone is sitting at the dining room table eating with the exception of Michael and Stevie. They are eating at the island in the kitchen because there isn't enough room for them at the dining room table. After dinner they have apple pie and chocolate cake for dessert. After dessert the girls clean up and everyone participates in one game of trivial pursuit. The game goes on for about two hours and finishes with Danielle and Gracie winning.

"That was fixed." Michael says.

"We won fair and square." Danielle replies followed by sticking her tongue out at Michael.

After the game everyone settles in the great room. They are drinking a little and enjoying the fire. The kids are watching Christmas DVD's. The night is so relaxing and enjoyable. By eleven o'clock Michael, Stevie and Maria are fast asleep. They are carried upstairs and put into bed.

"Who's going to midnight mass with Ryan and me?" Cheryl asks.

"I'm calling it a night and going home." Gracie replies.

"Randy and I are staying here with dad and kids." Jennifer replies.

"I'm going," Carol says.

"So am I," Greta replies.

So they get their coats on and head to St Anthony's in one car. Gracie's heads home after an exhausting day with limited cigarettes because she could only smoke outside. When they get to the church Ryan drops them off in front and he parks the car in the parking lot. He meets the girls inside and they sit in the middle of the church. Mass is forty minutes long and followed by communion as Father Angelo says the final prayer. As mass ends Father Angelo leads the procession out the front door where he greets all the parishioners as they leave.

"I'll go get the car. I will pick you up in front of the church so wait here." Ryan says as he walks into the dark parking lot.

Ryan walks towards the car and hits the unlock button.

"Excuse me sir." A voice says from the dark.

Before Ryan can say anything he is hit across the back of the head. Ryan falls to the ground unconscious. Todd leaves Ryan lying on the ground bleeding. He walks to the front of the church that is now cleared of parishioners. He rounds the corner and sees the three woman standing and waiting to be picked up. Cheryl turns her head and sees Todd walking towards her. She panics and starts to run in the opposite direction. Before Greta can say anything Todd punches her square in the face knocking her to the ground. Carol backs away but not before he pops her too. Cheryl tries to run away but she is wearing heels and dress. It's hard for her to move through the snow. Todd starts to run after her and easily catches up to her.

"Please, leave me alone." Cheryl yells as she runs down the snowy sidewalks.

"My life is over and so is yours." Todd yells back.

"If you don't leave me alone the deputies are here and they will not hesitate to shoot you." Cheryl yells trying to down grade Todd's demeanor.

"You mean the two deputies that are in the car right in front of you." Todd replies.

Cheryl looks up at both deputies in the car with their heads leaning against the windows. They are both knocked out and tied up.

"Wait until Ryan gets his hands on you." Cheryl says.

"He has to wake up first." Todd says as he starts to catch up to Cheryl.

Cheryl can see he is gaining on her so she darts towards the road. Before she can cross Todd grabs her by the arm. He throws her to the ground and then pulls her to her feet. He slaps her twice and pushes her against the farmer's pickup truck. Todd plays his cards right and Cheryl runs right toward his escape vehicle. Todd hits her two more times in the face cutting her lip open. Cheryl bleeds all over her long winter coat. Todd open the door to the pickup truck.

"Get in," Todd says in a rough and tough voice.

Cheryl looks down the road and she can see no one is coming to her rescue. Todd forcibly pushes her into passenger seat of the truck and that's when he belts her with a right knocking her out. Todd attaches her seat belt and he gets into the truck himself. He starts the truck and puts it into gear and starts to drive away.

Back at the church Carol is shaken up and crying hysterically. Greta is on her cell phone calling 911. Ryan is getting back to his feet and realizes what just happened. Without thinking Ryan jumps into his car and starts it up. He drives toward the exit of the parking lot just as Todd drives by. Ryan can see Cheryl lying against the passenger side window. Her eyes are closed and her face is bloodied. This sets Ryan off and puts his thought pattern in overdrive. He pulls out and follows the pickup truck. Ryan pulls out his cell phone and calls 911.

"911, what is your emergency?" A female voice says.

"This Ryan DeCicero and I'm following a pickup truck that has Todd LaRussa driving. He has apprehended his wife Cheryl so please approach with caution." Ryan says.

Ryan stays on the phone and gives the dispatcher directions as he follows the pickup. It takes Todd about a mile or so to realize that Ryan is following him. He tries twice to stop Ryan by slamming on the brakes. Ryan swerves both times to miss him but remains in pursuit with vengeance. The chase goes on for about ten minutes and that when Todd makes his mistake. He has two patrol car and Ryan following him as he tries to cross the Lake Ave Bridge. Todd races across the bridge just as the police block his path with five police cruisers.

"Son of a bitch." Todd yells as he slams on the brakes.

Todd turns the truck around in the opposite direction but it's too late. The police and Ryan have already blocked the other exit. Todd thinks about ramming through the blockade but that option is eliminated quickly because the police bring in two tractor trailers. They are parked behind the police cruisers on both sides of the bridge. Todd wants to make an example of this situation and he wants to kill Cheryl but not himself. A crash would probably kill both of them. Todd thinks hard as Cheryl begins to come around. Cheryl looks up and she can see the police officers converging on both sides of the bridge.

"Please Todd, let me go." Cheryl pleads

"Shut the hell up I'm trying to think here." Todd says in desperation.

"Please Todd, this doesn't have to end this way." Cheryl says.

Todd grabs Cheryl and pulls her over the console as he opens the driver's side door. Todd gets out of the truck and pulls Cheryl out of the truck like she is a rag doll.

"Let the girl go." A police officer says.

"I'll kill her if you don't back off." Todd yells like a riled maniac.

Todd drags Cheryl over to the guardrail of the bridge. He is pulling her with such force that he tears off her coat. Cheryl is yelling and screaming as Todd grabs her by the neck. He lifts her up and onto the top of the rail.

"If you don't back off I'm going to drop her off the edge." Todd screams frantically.

Cheryl looks down at the cold water moving below. Not only is the water cold but its thirty foot drop to the water. The police start to back off as Todd brings Cheryl back down to the ground. That is when Todd does the unexpected and wraps Cheryl's head against the metal bar of the guardrail. He hits her head with such force he knocks her out. Todd picks her up again but this time he has lifts her up over his head.

"No, do something!" Ryan yells.

Todd heaves Cheryl's unconscious body off the edge. Her body falls thirty feet into the icy cold water below. Todd laughs out loud like a raving lunatic. That's until he is hit with Tasers from both the left and the right side. Todd's body shakes uncontrollably as the electric current flows through his body.

"Oh no please lord don't do this to me." Ryan yells.

"This is your time my son." The old man says into Ryan's ear as he looks around and sees no one.

Ryan without thinking runs at full speed. He leaps the four foot guardrail fence and pushes off the top bar. Ryan uses the spot where Todd let Cheryl go as his reference. Ryan uses his momentum from the jump to dive off the thirty foot bridge. Ryan was an all American swimmer in high school and college. As Ryan plunges into the icy cold water below he makes a perfect dive. He goes down and under the water. It's dark and cold but Ryan's adrenaline is in full throttle. He searches under the water and swims hard while using his hands to reach out. Cheryl is unconscious and sinking to the bottom.

"We need emergency under water rescue team on the Lake Ave Bridge." A police officer says into his microphone.

Ryan swims and searches the area. He follows with the current as he is swept under the bridge. He comes up for air and goes back under the water. He continues to search but comes up with nothing. Ryan comes up for air again and then goes back under again. Then he feels something as he grabs onto it. He pulls that something to the surface. When he gets to the surface he pulls it up and out. Low and behold he snags Cheryl's arm. Ryan can tell she is not breathing but he has to get her out of the water before he can administer CPR. Ryan wraps his arm around Cheryl and swims to the river bank. The police can see him as they run down and around the side of the river to assist him. Ryan uses that adrenaline to fight off the cold and to get Cheryl to safety. It takes Ryan another two minutes to get Cheryl to the shore. The police are standing off to the side as they take Cheryl from Ryan and pull her to shore. Immediately they start CPR while rescue workers arrive on site. The rescue workers takes over and continues CPR as they carry Cheryl away on gurney. Cheryl is put into the back of the rescue truck. Ryan quickly strips out of his wet clothes and wraps a warming blanket around him. By the time Ryan gets to the street, he can see the rescue truck driving away.

"Oh God, please don't take her away from me. Please I'm begging you with all my heart." Ryan says as tears drip from his eyes.

Ryan looks up towards the bridge and he can see Todd being dragged into a police cruiser. Ryan can see the police set a few things straight with Todd because he was beaten beyond recognition.

"Come on, you need to be taken to the hospital to be evaluated." A paramedic says.

Ryan agrees and gets into to the second rescue truck. They drive to the hospital at the speed limit while the paramedic takes Ryan's vital signs. Ryan shivers in the blanket as the adrenaline rush wears off. Ryan lays on the gurney inside the rescue truck and can only think about Cheryl.

"Do you know how Cheryl is?" Ryan asks with his teeth chattering.

"I don't know, but she is in good hands. We will do our best." The paramedic replies as he takes Ryan's blood pressure.

The rescue truck ride is only six or seven minutes long. When they arrive at the hospital entrance the rescue truck parks by the emergency door. Then the back door opens in the rescue truck and Ryan is pulled out. They wheel him inside the hospital where he looks frantically for Cheryl. He passes a few emergency rooms as he looks inside them for Cheryl. Ryan is wheeled inside his own ER room where he sits and waits for a doctor to evaluate him. After a ten minute wait, a nurse walks in with some more warming blankets. Ryan is quick to pull off the other blanket as he stands there in his wet boxers.

"Is there any news on the girl that arrived before me?" Ryan asks.

"All I can tell you is they are working on her." The nurse replies.

The nurse takes Ryan's vital signs again. Ryan is beginning to warm up but he is worried about Cheryl.

"Would you like a pair of scrubs to change into?" The nurse asks as she starts to walk out the door.

"Yes please." Ryan answers.

Ryan continues to wait in the ER. The nurse returns with a pair of blue scrubs. Ryan quickly changes into the blue shirt and pants.

"We have a code blue in ER room seventeen." A female voice says over the intercom.

This sets Ryan's heart racing. He gets up off the bed and starts to walk towards the door. He opens the door and walks out into the ER hallway. Ryan moves from room to room peeking inside. When he reaches ER room six he can see doctors and nurses working frantically on a female patient. Ryan cannot see her face but he can tell it's a woman by her feet. Ryan tries to get closer when he is grabbed by a nurse and pulled out of the room.

"Is she going to be alright?" Ryan pleads to the nurse.

"Get back into you room. The hospital staff is working diligently to revive her." The nurse replies.

Ryan doesn't even want to look inside the room. His world is in ruins and he can't do anything more to prevent this heart break. With his head down and dejected Ryan walks at a slow pace towards his room.

"Hey," a female voice says in a low and faint tone from ER room thirteen.

Ryan looks up and inside the room. He sees Cheryl laying in the bed covered up in warming blankets. Her auburn hair is wet and hanging around her face and she is smiling at him.

"Oh my God, you're alive." Ryan says as he runs towards her.

Ryan wraps his arms around Cheryl who has tears running down her face. Ryan is filled with joy as he cannot let Cheryl go. They remain embraced for five minutes while they cry in each other's arms.

"I thought you were dead." Ryan whispers in Cheryl's ear.

"I was for a few minutes, but you reached me in time for the paramedics to revive me." Cheryl says as she hold on to Ryan for dear life.

"When they said code blue over the intercom I though my life was over." Ryan says to Cheryl.

"Ryan, I saw the light and started walking towards it. Then that old man I keep seeing stopped me and told me it wasn't my time yet." Cheryl says while she cries in Ryan's arms.

"I think he whispered in my ear to jump in the water and save you. He said to me this is your time my son." Ryan tells Cheryl.

"I am just so happy you were there. I can't imagine what my kids would have done if I died." Cheryl says while she weeps for joy.

"Let's not think about that. I love you." Ryan says.

"I love you too." Cheryl replies.

Both Cheryl and Ryan remain in the hospital until three thirty in the morning. The doctors wanted to make sure they were no complications from the exposure to the icy water. As they were leaving the hospital to go home on Christmas morning a police officer stood in the doorway.

 . "Your car is in the parking lot. We took the privilege to drop it off here. I am so glad to see both of you are alive and well. It is definitely a Christmas miracle I witnessed tonight." The police officer says to both Ryan and Cheryl.

"Thank you," Cheryl and Ryan reply together.

"By the way that dive off the Lake Ave Bridge put Tarzan to shame." The police officer says as they head out the door wearing scrubs.

Both Cheryl and Ryan laugh at the police officer comment. Cheryl and Ryan drive home together where everyone with the exception of the small children are waiting for them. Hugs and kisses are given as they walk into the door. By four fifteen everyone is in bed with the exception of Cheryl and Ryan. He helps Cheryl up to the master bedroom where Cheryl grabs onto Ryan and kisses him deeply and passionately.

"Now that Todd has been apprehended and Greta went home to sleep. I really don't feel like going to sleep right now." Cheryl says as she closes the door behind them.

Chapter 29 – Christmas Day

The next morning is Christmas Day. The kids are up at eight o'clock because they want to open their presents. Carol is up first so she makes a pot of coffee and starts breakfast. She is a little sore and bruised where Todd hit her. Slowly everyone gets out of bed and they make their way downstairs. The smell of coffee brewing and bacon cooking fills the house. Cheryl and Ryan are the last two downstairs. They both are sore and weary from the night before. Ryan's first stop is into the kitchen for a big cup of coffee.

"Can you get me a cup honey?" Cheryl asks Ryan.

"No problem." Ryan replies.

Everyone gathers in the great room by the Christmas tree. Presents are passed around and opened. Jennifer makes sure all the wrapping paper is disposed of as soon as a gifts is opened. Ryan and Cheryl sit on a couch as the kids have a wonderful and happy Christmas.

"I wonder what is in here. The label says it's from Santa." Michael says as he starts to open the gift.

Cheryl right off the bat doesn't recognize the wrapping paper. She turns and looks at Ryan with eyes like balls of fire.

"What did you buy him?" Cheryl asks while staring at Ryan.

"I didn't buy anything. Michael says it's from Santa." Ryan replies sarcastically.

"My ass it's from Santa." Cheryl whispers in Ryan's ear.

"Mom look, it's an Xbox One! Yes, it's all I ever wanted." Michael says jumping up and down.

Ryan spent a lot of money on all four kids. When Danielle opens her gift she is ecstatic to see the iPhone and hugs both Ryan and Cheryl.

"Thank you, thank you, thank you." Danielle says as she turns on the cell phone.

"Hey mom this one is for you." Michael says as he hands Cheryl the small box.

Cheryl opens the box with anticipation. When she opens the lid on the jewelry box she is in shock. All the years married to Todd, he never ever gave her a piece of jewelry.

"Oh my god it's beautiful, Thank you so much." Cheryl says as she pull out the heart shaped pendant and necklace.

Cheryl kisses Ryan on the lips and then puts the necklace on. After all the gifts are opened everyone sits down to eat breakfast. Bacon, eggs and toast with coffee and juice. The main topic of conversation is last night's drama that unfolded after midnight mass. Then Ryan remembers, there is one more gift that he left in the garage. He gets up from the dining room table and starts to walk towards the garage.

"Where are you going?" Cheryl asks.

"I forgot something in the garage from yesterday." Ryan says as he walks out the door and into the garage.

Within a minutes or so Ryan returns with a box. Danielle and Michael look at each other with a puzzled look because the box is making whimpering sounds.

"This is for you guys to open." Ryan says as he hands the box to Danielle and Michael to open.

The box is quiet large in size with big holes in the top. Danielle has a hard time holding the box because whatever is inside is moving. Michael and Danielle can see a black wet nose peeping through the holes in the top of the box. Danielle sets the box on the floor and pulls the top off. Out pops an eight week old golden retriever.

"He is a fluff ball." Carol says as the dog runs around the floor wagging his tail and sniffing everyone.

"Really now, where am I going to put that dog when we move in the spring." Cheryl says with her hands on her hips.

"Nowhere." Dan says from the head of the table.

"What are you talking about?" Cheryl says as she looks over at Ryan.

Ryan just stands there with a smirk on his face.

"Well Carol and I have been thinking that this trip up north and how it's getting to be so hard on us. This is such a beautiful house only to be occupied but for a few months a year. We decided that we are signing the house over to you and Ryan." Dan says.

Cheryl breaks down and starts to cry. Ryan walks over and wraps his arms around Cheryl. Danielle and Michael are yelling and screaming for joy. The dog is running around eating all the scraps that have fallen on the floor. It's a joyous Christmas day for the entire family.

Dinner is served and the lasagna with homemade sauce is a hit. The whole family including Gracie and Greta are there as they enjoy the holiday meal together.

"Here, here, a toast to the most memorable Christmas and to a wonderful family." Cheryl says with her wine glass in the air.

Everyone clicks their glasses together and sips their wine.

"I would like to wish everyone a Merry Christmas." Carol say with a big smile on her face.

"Merry Christmas." Everyone replies together.

"And to all a good night." Michael says laughing.

Dinner goes over well as expected. Dessert consists of homemade cream puffs and éclairs. By seven in the evening Greta is getting her coat on to go home. Ryan and Cheryl walk her to the door.

"I'm just glad this whole ordeal with Todd is over. Thank you for your hospitality. I love both you guys" Greta says as she kisses Cheryl of the cheek.

"You're welcome here anytime." Cheryl replies as Greta heads out the door.

Ryan and Cheryl walk back into the great room holding hands. Michael and Stevie are playing the Lego game on the Xbox. They are yelling and having fun as Danielle keeps telling them to keep the noise down while she is on the phone. By seven thirty Gracie gets ready to go home. Ryan retrieves her coat from the coat rack in the foyer. Ryan helps her put on her coat as Cheryl unlocks the front door.

"Cheryl I am truly sorry for what my son has done to you. I will do everything in my power to help you and the children. I can't apologize any more for own actions and the way I treated you. Mark my words it will never happen again. Just don't take the kids out of my life." Gracie says with tears in her eyes.

"Gracie, it's just water under the bridge. I know you love the kids and you were just trying to protect your son. I will never keep them away from their grandmother." Cheryl says as she hugs her ex mother-in-law.

"Thank you so very much." Gracie says as she heads out the door to her car.

Cheryl closes the door and watches as Gracie walks on the snow towards her car. Cheryl stays there to make sure Gracie gets into her car safely. Gracie gets in and starts the car. She puts the car in gear and starts to drive away. She sees Cheryl looking out the window and waves to her. Cheryl waves back with a smile on her face.

By eight o'clock Randy, Jennifer and the kids are getting an early head start on a long drive. Randy likes to drive through the night because there is a lot less traffic on the roads. Cheryl and Ryan help them load the car and get the kids situated. Cheryl gets Maria into her car seat while Jennifer tends to Stevie. Ryan and Randy get all the luggage into the trunk of the car.

"You know my brother is in love with you. I can see it in his eyes that you and the children are his world." Jennifer says to Cheryl.

"I know and I'm in love with him. He has been there for me and he treats my children like they are his" Cheryl says to Jennifer inside the car.

"Treat him like gold Cheryl. He is one in a million." Jennifer says as she gets into the front passenger seat.

"Have a safe trip home and call us when you get there." Cheryl says to Jennifer as they hug each other.

"We will and please don't break his heart." Jenifer whispers in Cheryl ear.

"I won't." Cheryl whispers back.

Randy and Ryan shakes hands. Randy gets into the car and starts to drive off. They wave goodbye to each other as the car heads down the driveway. Cheryl and Ryan walk together towards the house with their arms wrapped around each other.

"It was a good Christmas." Cheryl says as they walk up the steps on the front porch.

"It was a great Christmas. I wouldn't have it any other way. Oops scratch that I might change a few things from last night." Ryan says as he kisses Cheryl.

They head back inside the house and go over the fireplace to warm up. The television is on with a *Christmas Carol* starring *George C Scott*. The only lights emitting were from the Christmas tree and fireplace. Carol and Dan are sitting on the couch on the left. Danielle and Michael are sitting on the couch on the right. They are mesmerized with the movie as Cheryl rubs her dress up and down to warm up by the fire.

"It's a little cold out there." Carol says.

"Yea just a tad." Cheryl replies.

Ryan looks over at Cheryl while he is trying to warm up also. He can see in her eyes that look of love as she gazes at him. Ryan was going to wait until later but he can't hold back the anticipation.

"It was an eventful and emotional day with a lot of surprises. Thank you mom and dad for giving us the house. I don't know what to say about that act of generosity. To you Cheryl LaRussa, you really had me scared last night. I thought I was going to lose you and I find that unacceptable. I love you and your children like they are my own. I am truly in love with you and I was wondering if you would spend the rest of your life with me." Ryan says as he goes down on one knee in front of his mom, dad and Cheryl's children.

There Ryan presented Cheryl with a family heirloom diamond. The marque cut diamond that was his grandmothers. Ryan had the diamond reset in a brand new gold setting. The one and a half karat diamond glistens with the firelight from the fireplace. Cheryl looks down at the diamond with a tear forming in her eyes. Carol, Dan and the children look on with puppy dog eyes waiting for Cheryl's answer.

"I have only been divorced for nine days. I don't think I can make a commitment into marriage so soon. But since you are a once in a life time find how can I say no. Yes, yes, yes I would love to marry you." Cheryl says as Ryan gets to his feet and kisses his bride to be.

Carol and Dan remain seated and hold each other's hand. They were ecstatic that they were gaining a daughter-in-law and two new grandchildren. Most of all they were happy for their son because he worshiped Cheryl since they were in grade school together. To finally see Ryan's dream come true was a prayer answered.

Danielle and Michael were over joyed because for once they have a father figure that cares about them. Even though they love their father, Todd was never a father figure. He only thought about himself and what would benefit him.

That night everyone went to bed without fear. Todd was in custody and that felt like a weight being lifted off everyone's shoulders. Ryan and Cheryl made love for a second night in a row. They are truly in love with each other and it shows in their eyes. After their love making session they went to sleep. At three in the morning Cheryl is wakened by a sound. She gets up and walks into the hallway upstairs. There the old man is standing but his image is glowing like a ghost.

"Who are you?" Cheryl asks.

"Who do you think I am?" The old man replies.

"You are my guardian angel." Cheryl responds.

"You could say that Cheryl. I am the heavenly image of who was once your father." The old man say as he changes his image to Cheryl's fathers face.

"Oh my god dad, I have missed you so much." Cheryl says with tears in her eyes.

"I have watched over you since the day I left the earth. I see the pain you have endured over the years. The heavenly father heard your prayers and saved you from the incident on the bridge last night." The old man's says with sincerity.

"I was supposed to die last night?" Cheryl asks.

"I cannot answer that question. The heavenly father has seen your pain and watched you sacrifice for your children. My child you must always believe and pray because he is listening. I must go now, my job is done here." The old man replies.

"Dad, can't you stay." Cheryl pleads.

"I will be here, you just won't be able to see me. I love you and I am proud of the woman you have become." The old man says as his image fades away.

"Dad, dad, dad," Cheryl yells from her bed as she awakes from a deep sleep.

"Are you alright honey?" Ryan says as he turns on the light on the nightstand.

"I'm fine, I was just dreaming." Cheryl replies.

Ryan turns off the light and rolls over on his back to sleep. Cheryl lays on her back and looks into the hallway. She thinks to herself, was this a dream or her mental emotions working in overdrive. Cheryl wants to believe it was real as she looks into the hallway again. There she sees a glowing light fade away and disappear. Cheryl smiles to herself and closes her eyes.

"Good night daddy and thank you and the lord for helping me in my time of need. I love my family and the people in my life. I am truly blessed." Cheryl says to herself with her hands folded like she is praying.

Chapter 30 – Happily Ever After

The Christmas holiday passes and Carol and Dan fly back to Florida. Cheryl doesn't tell Ryan about dream of the old man being her father and guardian angel. They live together in harmony until their wedding day on Saturday June 28th. All family members fly in for the wedding. It's only a small wedding with just family and close friends. Cheryl even asks Dan if he would give her away and he is more than happy to. They have the ceremony outside in front of the Inn on the Lake. The reception will be held inside for a party of thirty-five. Before everything gets started Cheryl and Ryan are together and dressed. Cheryl is wearing a knee high white dress with lace at the hem and bodice. The neckline is dressed with pearls and gems. Ryan is dressed in a black tuxedo, white shirt and black shoes. They stand together with less than a half an hour until the ceremony. Guests and family are arriving while they talk by the pond in front of the arch they will be married under.

"You look a little nervous?" Cheryl asks Ryan.

"Yea just a little. How can you tell?" Ryan replies with beads of sweat forming on his forehead.

"Because you sweating and you don't sweat very often." Cheryl says with a smile.

"Is it that obvious?" Ryan asks.

"You will be fine just do as we rehearsed last night." Cheryl says.

They watch as the guests start to gather in front of the restaurant.

"That dress looks absolutely stunning on you." Ryan say to Cheryl.

"Thank you, you don't look too bad yourself." Cheryl says as she takes Ryan by the hand with a look of concern on her face.

"What's wrong honey, is there something bothering you?" Ryan says as he puts his other hand over the top of Cheryl's.

"I have something to ask you." Cheryl says as she looks down at the ground.

"What is it? You better hurry because the crowd is beginning to flock our way." Ryan says.

"Do you like my children?" Cheryl asks with her brown eyes making contact with Ryan eyes.

"Why would that question even come up? I love and adore your children like they're my own." Ryan states as he squeezes Cheryl's hand showing his love.

"Because I'm pregnant and I'm going to have our baby." Cheryl says with a stream of tears dripping down her face.

"Oh my god, are you kidding me!" Ryan replies ecstatically as he wraps his arms around his bride to be.

"You're not mad." Cheryl says as she cries while she embraces Ryan.

"No way I'm mad at you. I love you for who you are. I always wanted a family I just never found the right person to spend my life with. I love you, Danielle, Michael and the baby and nothing is ever going to change that." Ryan says with enthusiasm.

"I love you too." Cheryl says she kisses him on the neck.

"What is it a boy or girl?" Ryan whispers in Cheryl's ear as the guest begin to gather.

"I don't know yet, I'm only four weeks pregnant." Cheryl whispers.

"Let's keep it our secret until we get back for our honeymoon." Ryan whispers.

"I love you and I don't know what I would do without you." Cheryl whisper.

"Let's get this show on the road." Randy say as he walks down to get Ryan because he is the best man.

The wedding is a big hit with good food, good music and good company. Everyone drinks in excess with the exception of the bride who only has one glass of champagne. At the end of the reception everyone departs the hall and Carol takes Cheryl aside.

"You made a beautiful bride and I know my son loves you with all his heart. There is one thing that I noticed and that is your radiant beauty. Which only shows when you're expecting. I can keep a secret if you can." Carol says with love and tenderness.

Tears well in Cheryl's eyes and Carol dabs them with her handkerchief. Cheryl can't hold back and embraces her new mother-in-law. Cheryl never had an extended family that ever showed her love. This was something she can easily adapt too.

After the wedding they spend their honeymoon in Florida. One week in Disney World with the kids. One week at the beach with the kids and Ryan's parents. The third week Ryan and Cheryl go on a cruise by themselves. Danielle and Michael stay with Carol and Dan at their home.

On another note, Todd is found guilty of numerous felonies including murder in the second degree, extortion, kidnapping, attempted kidnapping, aggravated assault, attempted murder and so on and so forth. He is sentenced to life in prison without parole. His girlfriend Prudence was found guilty of being an accessory to Todd in ten different counts and she is serving fifty years.

On February 26th Daniel Ryan DeCicero was born to Cheryl and Ryan. He is nineteen inches long and weighs seven pounds three ounces. Ryan is still working as a lawyer and Cheryl is now a stay at home mom. Danielle helps her mother in every way possible with the new baby. She spends every waking moment she can with him. Michael on the other hand is just like any other nine year old playing games on the Xbox. He could care less about the baby as long as he has a controller in his hand.

The DeCicero family is living in harmony and love as they live happily ever after.

For more stories by Frank Cereo please visit his website
www.frankcereo.com